A DEADLY DIVIDEND

A gripping murder mystery set in Dublin

DAVID PEARSON

THE BOOK FOLKS

Paperback edition published by

The Book Folks

London, 2020

© David Pearson

ISBN 978-1-913516-90-1

www.thebookfolks.com

To Andrew,
for being so supportive over such a long time

Chapter One

"Jesus, Mary, there's someone at the door."

Pat turned over and saw that the little green figures on the bedside clock said 2:40. Mary, his wife, continued to sleep, or at least feign sleep, in the bed beside him, as he threw back the blankets and struggled to put on his slippers.

"Who the hell can that be at this hour of night?" Pat grumbled. He was up now, and beginning to focus. He went to the bedroom door where his dressing gown was hanging on a hook, and wrapped it hurriedly around himself. Thump, thump – there it was again – a determined effort to wake the household coming from downstairs.

"It's probably John after forgetting his keys again," Mary said sleepily from the comfort of the double bed.

Pat grunted as he made his way carefully down the steep, narrow stairs in the little terraced house. He took the steps gingerly. His arthritis was at him again, and the last thing he needed was a fall.

When he got downstairs, he switched on the lights, which revealed a dark shape on the other side of the glass-panelled front door. Pat opened it just a little, being not quite sure what to expect.

"Mr McKenna?" said the tall, lanky Garda standing outside on the footpath. His female colleague, much shorter in stature, looked on silently.

"Yes, I'm Pat McKenna. How can I help you?"

"May we come in please, sir?" the female officer said.

"Oh, right. Yes, sure, come in," Pat said, standing aside and indicating that the two should go into the front room to the left of the narrow hallway.

The room was tidy, but small, with a slightly tired looking sofa, an easy chair in front of a tiled fireplace, and a densely patterned floral carpet in autumn colours on the floor. Pat switched on the single light in the room which was suspended from the centre of the ceiling and bore a plastic shade that had a good amount of dust accumulated on it.

"Sit ye down there," Pat said.

The two officers sat on the worn, brown moquette covered sofa, close to the edge of the seat. They didn't want to appear in any way relaxed.

"My name is Garda Richard Walsh, and this is my colleague, Emily O'Connor," the tall Garda said, removing his cap and gesturing towards his companion.

"Can I ask if you have a son called John, Mr McKenna?" Walsh said.

"John, yes, of course. He's a fine lad."

"Can you tell us where he is just now, sir?"

"Well, if he's not upstairs in bed, then he's still out with some of his pals. They keep funny hours, you know, these young folks."

"I wonder if you could just check upstairs for us, Mr McKenna?" Garda O'Connor said.

"Well, righto. But what's all this about? What's going on?"

"If you could just check his room for us, please, Mr McKenna," O'Connor said.

"OK, so. Wait there then," Pat said rather unnecessarily.

He got up from his chair, now feeling apprehensive, and disappeared out the door. The Gardaí could hear the man climbing the stairs slowly. They said nothing, but exchanged a knowing glance.

When Pat McKenna reappeared, his wife was with him. Introductions were hurriedly exchanged, and then Mary slipped quickly into her normal hospitable role.

"Can I get you a cup of tea?" she said.

"No thanks, we're grand, Mrs McKenna. Is John upstairs then?" the Garda said.

"No, he's not in yet. There must be a party on somewhere. Why do want to know about John anyway?" Pat said.

"Well, a young man who we believe may be your son has been injured in town. He's been taken to St James's," Garda Walsh said.

"Oh, dear God almighty. Is he OK? What happened?" Mary said, wringing her hands, her voice now an octave higher.

"That's all the information we have for now, Mrs McKenna, but if you like, we can give you a lift to the hospital," the female officer said.

"What happened? And why do you think it's John?" Pat McKenna said.

"We found his driving license in his wallet," Walsh said.

"Is he OK, Garda? You haven't said what happened. For God's sake, tell us how he is!" Pat said.

"Best if you just come along with us. Put some clothes on, and we'll go. Don't forget your keys so you can get back in."

* * *

At the hospital, the two Gardaí spoke quietly to the nurse in charge of the accident and emergency admissions desk. The place was jammed with the night's casualties, and there was an associated hubbub of conversations, so the Gardaí were able to talk to the nurse without being overheard. Garda Walsh nodded towards the two elderly parents, who looked worried and distraught as they waited for some news of their eldest child. Then, Mary and Pat were shown into a small room and asked to wait. They tried in vain to get some information about their injured son, but none was forthcoming.

Finally, the door to the room where Pat and Mary were waiting opened with a flourish, and a young Indian doctor with a white coat and stethoscope around his neck came in.

"Mr and Mrs McKenna?" he said.

"Yes, Pat and Mary, that's right," Pat said hopefully, standing up as he did so.

"Please, take a seat," the doctor said, gesturing to the rather basic chairs scattered around the small room.

"Your son, John, was brought in about forty-five minutes ago, and I've been working on him ever since. He was very badly injured, I'm afraid. We did all we could for him, Mr McKenna, but I'm afraid it was no good. I'm sorry to say, we pronounced him dead within the last few minutes. I'm really sorry. Would you like me to get someone to come and stay with you? I'm sorry, but I have to get back – we're very busy tonight."

Pat McKenna put his arm around his wife's shoulder as she dissolved into uncontrollable sobbing. After a few minutes, the doctor departed, and was replaced by a ward sister.

"Can we see him?" Pat asked when she had introduced herself and expressed her sympathy.

"Yes, yes of course. Give us a few minutes just to tidy up. I'll come back and get you."

Chapter Two

Detective Inspector Aidan Burke had been asleep for just over two hours when his iPhone started to vibrate on his bedside table. Despite being in quite a deep sleep, a combination of the vibration and the light from the phone eventually penetrated his slumber, and he reached out from under the covers, groping for the device.

"Burke," he croaked.

"Inspector Burke, sorry to disturb you, sir, this is Sergeant Doyle. We've had a report of a stabbing in the laneway at the back of Beresford Place. The ambulance has taken the victim up to St James's, and there are two uniformed Gardaí at the scene. They think the lad that was stabbed is in a bad way. He may not make it, so they've requested a senior officer to attend."

"Bugger! What time is it anyway?" Burke said.

"Just after two-thirty, sir."

"For fuck sake! OK, get a couple more men out to help secure the location. I'll be there in fifteen minutes. Make sure the scene is preserved. Oh, and have you got forensics out?"

"Yes, sir. They're on their way."

Burke's mouth felt as if it was full of sand, and he knew his breath stank, almost certainly as a result of the several pints of Guinness and the few Irish whiskeys he had imbibed earlier in the night at McGroarty's pub in Crumlin, close to where he lived. Lesser men would still be drunk after such a quantity of alcohol, but Burke was well used to it, and his corpulent form was able to absorb large amounts of drink on a regular basis while he remained, apparently, fairly sober.

He dressed into the same creased white shirt and crumpled grey suit that he had taken off not long before, and ran warm water over his rugged face in the bathroom before grabbing his keys and leaving the small, terraced house that he called home these days.

Burke was separated. He had married at the age of twenty-six, but by the time he reached forty his wife, Deirdre, had become completely fed up with his constant absence and heavy drinking, and she had kicked him out. Deirdre had retained the family home in the fashionable suburbs in Knocklyon, while he just managed to keep a second mortgage going on the house in Crumlin which he had bought cheaply, in poor repair, the condition of which had not improved much under his care.

The early morning traffic heading into town was sparse. It was largely comprised of taxis coming and going to and from the various late bars that were still open, providing a lucrative trade for the 'night men' as they were known. It only took Burke twelve minutes to get to Beresford Place where he stopped his Volkswagen Passat in front of the cordon that had been set up by the uniformed Gardaí.

"Good morning, sir," the young Garda manning the cordon said as Burke approached.

"Do ye think it is now? Maybe it's good for you, but not for the poor bugger who was stabbed. What's your name anyway?" Burke said gruffly.

"Brennan, sir. Dermot Brennan."

"Well, Dermot Brennan, I'd better get in here and see what's what, don't you think?"

Brennan lifted the tape up high enough to let Burke pass beneath it, glad that the senior officer was moving away. He was clearly in a bad mood.

Burke walked down the dark, narrow alleyway behind the shops and pubs that each had rear doors opening onto the fetid lane. Overflowing bins and bags of rubbish, carelessly tied up and spilling over, stood at both sides of the little street like tired sentries. A white tent had been erected where the victim had been found, and there were already two officers in white scene-of-crime suits bent down gathering evidence from the floor.

Burke recognised one of the men.

"Jim. What have we got so far?"

"Hello, Aidan. Jesus, you're looking a bit rough. Hard night, was it?"

"You're not looking so handy yourself, Jim. Now what's the story here?" Burke said.

"We don't know much yet. A young fella was found by one of the barmen from the pub just here when he was putting out the rubbish. He'd been stabbed and he was bleeding all over the place. The barman called Store Street, and when the lads got here they identified the victim as John McKenna from his driving license. They got the ambulance out and he was taken off to St James's. But it doesn't look good, he was well cut up, apparently."

"Have we taken a statement from the barman?"

"Now, that would be your job, Aidan. I'm just trying to get some evidence here."

"And what exactly have you got so far?"

"Bugger nothing – so far. But we've only been here a few minutes. Give us a bit of time. Though with all the shit around here on the street, I wouldn't get your hopes up too much."

Burke left the tent and went to the back door of the bar that was standing ajar, the fug of the place wafting out into the cool morning air. Inside, he found two men seated at a table with what looked like brandy in front of them.

"Which one of you boyos found the lad then?" Burke said.

"I... I did," one of the men volunteered.

He was a small, wiry youth, probably no more than twenty or twenty-two years old, dressed in a black T-shirt and black jeans with a plastic card dangling around his neck on a lanyard. He had short dark hair, cut tight to the sides of his head, and a tattoo on his left forearm.

"What's your name then?" Burke said, addressing the lad.

"Conor Griffin, sir."

"Well, Conor, why don't you tell me all about it? And, yes, I'd love a drop of brandy – just to keep out the cold, don't you know."

The second barman jumped up and went behind the bar to fetch a generous measure of the spirit for Burke, who had taken out his pocket book and pen and was waiting for Griffin to tell his tale.

"We had finished in here, and I was tidying up, getting ready for tomorrow. There was a full bag of rubbish for the bins, so I went out into the lane with it."

"What time would this have been?" Burke asked.

"Around twenty past one. We close up at one, and by the time I had the rubbish collected, it would have been about twenty past. It wasn't too busy tonight – the rain kept the crowds away. I had dropped the bag beside our bins, and turned to come back in when I saw him. He was just lying there. I knew he was badly hurt, like."

"Did he say anything to you?"

"No, not a word. I went across to him, but he was out of it, just clutching his stomach. And there was a lot of blood. So I came back in here and called 999, didn't I, Colin?" Griffin said.

"Yeah, that's right. You were proper pale too, like you'd seen a ghost," the other barman said, taking a good swig of his drink.

"Did you see anyone else in the lane, Conor?"

"No, no one. Just people passing by at the end of the alley. But they weren't looking or stopping or nothing."

"Is there any CCTV outside there?"

"Not bloody likely. Sure, wouldn't it be nicked as soon as it was put up? There's nothing like that."

"Did you touch the man at all – his clothes or anything?"

"No fear. I was scared out of me wits. I never seen anything like that."

"Was the man that was injured a customer? Had you ever seen him in here at all?"

"No, I never seen him before, honest. Will he be OK?"

"I don't know, Conor. I'm going up to the hospital just now when we're finished here. Has anything like this ever happened around here that you can remember?"

"No, I don't think so. Ye hear things and all, but I never seen anything myself. Not like that."

"Right. We'll leave it at that for now. Here – just write your name and address in my notebook. You'll need to come into the station tomorrow and make a statement. Ask for Detective Sergeant Moore, she'll look after it. OK? And thanks for the drink," Burke said, holding up the glass of brandy before draining it in one go.

Burke collected his notebook, glancing at the address the barman had written in it. He folded it and put it away, and left again by the same back door.

"Well, Jim, anything yet?" he said to Jim Roberts.

"Not much, Aidan. A few footprints that might be from the perpetrator's shoes, or maybe not."

"What about his phone?"

"Haven't found one yet. Maybe the killer took it, or it may be around here somewhere amongst all this crap. Or in a drain," Jim said, gesturing to the many black refuse sacks piled up in the alleyway.

"Any sign of a weapon?"

"Not yet – but we haven't emptied the bins. You wouldn't like to lend a hand with that, I presume?"

"You presume correctly, Jim. I have to go up to the hospital to see the victim. I'll leave you to your work, but let me know if you find anything, won't you?"

"Yes, of course. Good night, or should that be good morning?"

Chapter Three

Burke drove back up along the quays and round by the front of Trinity College, turning right into Dame Street and on up through Lord Edward Street, Thomas Street, and into the large hospital complex known as St James's Memorial Hospital at Usher's Island. The sprawling maze of buildings and porta-cabins had started life in 1603 when Dublin Corporation purchased the site for a poor house. Building on the site didn't actually commence till one hundred years later, and while it went through several iterations of different types of infant hospitals from 1703 to the early twentieth century, it wasn't until 1921 that it became a recognised and fully functional hospital, then known as St Kevin's. The name was changed in 1971, and since that time it has become the largest teaching hospital in Ireland, and been chosen for the location of the new National Children's Hospital, completing, as it were, a full circle from its early years.

Burke abandoned his car at the main entrance, leaving a Garda sign clearly visible in the front windscreen of his rather dilapidated VW, and went inside in search of the young victim.

After a few false starts, and a frustrating amount of waiting around which didn't sit easy on the impatient detective, he was introduced to Dr Patel, the doctor who had attended John McKenna when he was admitted.

"What can you tell me about the lad?" Burke asked. They were seated in a small ante-room where a nurse had managed to produce some quite drinkable coffee for them both.

"Just the usual sort of thing, Inspector. He was brought in by ambulance at, let me see, 1:57 a.m., bleeding heavily from two deep stab wounds to the front of his torso. One of the wounds nicked the pulmonary artery, and I'm afraid from that point on, he was doomed. We did all the usual things, but he'd lost a lot of blood and his heart had stopped either at the scene or in the ambulance. There was nothing I could do."

"I see. And have you any idea what kind of weapon might have been used, Doctor?"

"That will be for the post-mortem to discover, Inspector. I just try to keep them alive, and when that doesn't work, the pathologists take over."

"Have you had any other stabbings in tonight?"

"No – at least not yet, thank God. There's a few bloody noses and black eyes from various punch ups, but nothing as bad as this," Patel said.

"Right. I'd better let you get on. Are there any relatives in for him?"

"Yes. His mother and father are in one of the visitors' rooms. The nurse will show you."

"Terrific! Thanks, Doc."

Burke walked down through what seemed like endless corridors, inhaling the pungent odour of disinfectant and cleaning material, accompanied by a pretty young nurse in a blue uniform. He didn't like hospitals. Eventually they arrived at a door with a frosted glass panel, marked J-205, and the nurse gestured for Burke to go inside.

Pat and Mary McKenna were sitting beside each other, holding hands, looking down at the floor in a dejected state. They had both been crying, and looked pale and drawn.

"Mr and Mrs McKenna – my name is Detective Inspector Aidan Burke. May I say how sorry I am for your loss. This is a terrible business altogether. Is there anyone that can come in to be with you?"

Pat McKenna just shook his head.

"I'm sorry to have to trouble you at this time, but if you're up to it, I need to ask you a few questions," Burke said, tentatively. He started with some very basic, easy ones.

"Can I ask when you last saw your son? John, isn't it?"

"He came home as usual after work yesterday at around half past six. He lives with us, you know. He's saving up to buy a place with his girlfriend. Mary will surely miss him when he moves out, he's a great help to her these days, especially when she's poorly. Anyway, he had his dinner, and then changed his clothes and went out soon after eight. He said he was going into town to meet some mates," Pat McKenna said, having regained some of his composure.

"Did he mention any names at all, or where in town he was headed?"

"No, but it was probably Fintan and Tom. Those are his best buddies, and they usually hang around together," Mary said.

"Does he work with these two?"

"Yes, at the bank. They're all in the bank – you know, the big one with its offices on Hatch Street up beyond the Concert Hall, opposite the Iveagh Gardens."

"Do you know these lads' surnames?" Burke said.

Mary McKenna looked at her husband, and he replied, "Fintan is Fintan O'Loughlin, and I think Tom is Tom Keogh: yes, that's it, Keogh. His father owns a garage out on the Naas Road somewhere."

"And did John say specifically where he was meeting Tom and Fintan this evening?" Burke said.

"No, no he didn't. I don't know the places that the young folks get to these days. It's all new to me. When I was a young fella the pubs all closed at half-eleven, or eleven in the winter. Now they seem to stay open all night. And the Holy Hour is gone altogether," McKenna said, referring to the old Dublin licensing laws that saw the pubs closing between two-thirty and three-thirty in the afternoon for many years.

"I don't suppose you know where these two friends of John's live, do you?" Burke said.

"Tom still lives with his folks up somewhere near Rathfarnham, but Fintan has his own apartment over near Grand Canal Dock, I think," Mary McKenna said.

"Did John have a car?" Burke said.

The reference to their son in the past tense set Mary McKenna off again, so her husband answered, "No, no he didn't. We don't have any parking at home, and in any case, we're so close to everything he didn't need one. Tom has a car, of course, and they used to use his if they needed to go out of town."

"Well, thank you both very much. I'll leave you in peace now. Would it be OK if I came around tomorrow and had a quick look in John's bedroom? It might help us sort this out."

"Yes, of course, Inspector. Do you think you will catch whoever did this?" Pat McKenna asked.

"I certainly hope so, Mr McKenna. I really do."

Burke thought it was a bit odd that a relatively prosperous young man should still be living at home in his late twenties, but when he thought about it a bit more, he said to himself, "Ah, lads and their mammies. It's always the same!"

Chapter Four

Burke arrived in the Garda Station in central Dublin soon after nine o'clock in the morning. On the way home during the early hours, he had left a number of voicemails, but badly needed to get some more sleep before he was in any condition to deal with this new case.

Detective Sergeant Fiona Moore was at her desk. She had received Burke's voicemail as soon as she turned on her phone at breakfast, and was now busy putting a few pieces of information together to start the investigation. Moore had joined the force some five years earlier with the intention of starting a career and finding a husband, or if not a husband, at least a stable life partner. She had been quite unsuccessful with boys during her teenage years, being a little plump and not terribly good-looking. She had even struggled to find a partner for her debs' dance in the final year of school, although she eventually managed to snag a spotty youth that no one else wanted. But even he took off about an hour into the party, and she hadn't seen him since.

Moore was very close to her mother, and they often discussed her threadbare love life.

"What you need, Fee," her mother would say, "is to get into the Guards. Plenty of solid hard-working men there, and they are good providers too."

So, Fiona Moore had taken her mother's advice to heart, and joined the force with the objective of nabbing one of these fine, upstanding, hard-working providers. Her mother had also helped her to improve her appearance, letting her dark chestnut-coloured hair grow, and getting her to lose several pounds, so that now she presented a better prospect.

She had succeeded quite early on in attracting the attention of an older member of the force, and they became romantically involved. Unfortunately, unbeknownst to Fiona, the man was already married with three children, and in any case was transferred to Cork after some questions arose about the disappearance of a number of valuable electrical items that were the proceeds of a robbery. Fiona viewed this as a significant setback, but was still undeterred in her quest, although she also had to admit that the work was more appealing than she had imagined, and she now quite enjoyed her job as a detective sergeant, not that working alongside Aidan Burke was easy. She kept reassuring herself that at just twenty-eight years of age, she was in no danger of being left on the shelf, and after her first early experience, she was in no hurry to start another relationship that might end in tears.

"Morning, sir," she said.

"Is it? Bloody thing had me up half the night. What have you got so far, if anything?" Burke said.

"Well, not much. But I've started logging names – you know, the lads from the bar; the victim's friends and so on. We need all of the lad's known associates, though, to complete the picture."

"And?"

"We wouldn't be that lucky," Moore replied.

"It's all bollocks, anyway. C'mon, get your jacket. We're going out."

Moore knew better than to question her boss when he was in this kind of humour. They got on well, despite the fact that they had very different personalities, and worked in very different ways. Somehow, the unlikely mixture worked, and they were known for getting results, even if it was often by unconventional means.

On the way down to the car, Moore asked, "Where are we going, boss?"

"You'll see. I'm driving."

Burke drove through the busy city streets where the morning rush hour was just subsiding into the normal nightmare of Dublin's traffic. Dublin's thoroughfares hadn't been widened since Victorian times, and since then the volume of cars, buses, lorries and bicycles had multiplied a hundred-fold or more. Then the City Council decided to introduce Quality Bus Corridors where only buses and taxis could legitimately drive – that was before cycle lanes became fashionable, and once they were installed, many arteries were reduced to just one lane for cars. The *coup de grâce* had been the installation of hundreds of sets of traffic lights at every intersection, and even some where there was no apparent reason for them, making sure that motorists' progress through the town was normally slower than walking pace.

Burke cursed as they edged along until they got to Earlsfort Terrace where things improved somewhat. He turned into Hatch Street and pulled the car up outside the offices of the National Bank, stopping on double yellow lines, and the pair got out.

They entered the impressive edifice through a rotating glass door and were almost immediately confronted by a bank of desks where three receptionists and a rather burly security guard with a shaved head and a mean looking expression were posted.

"Good morning, sir," the first girl said, ignoring Moore completely. "How can I help you?"

"I need to see whoever's in charge of John McKenna. I understand he works here."

"I'm sorry, sir. We couldn't possibly give out that sort of information. It's against our security policy," the girl said frostily. Moore noticed that the security guard had perked up, perhaps in anticipation of some action to punctuate his boring day.

Burke produced his warrant card, leaned over the desk and, bringing his face to within inches of the girl, said, "Look here, missy. John McKenna was found in the early hours on the floor in an alleyway not too far from here, his lifeblood leaking out of him onto the cold wet concrete after he had been stabbed in the gut. I'm the poor bugger that's supposed to find his killer. So, don't piss me off with your policy nonsense, OK? Just get me McKenna's manager, and now would be a good time."

The receptionist flinched visibly at the news, and went very pale. She consulted her computer and made a phone call. When she had finished, she turned to Burke and said, "Mr Giltrap will be down in a moment, Inspector Burke. If you'd just like to take a seat." The girl got up and, holding a tissue to her face, dashed off to the bathroom sobbing.

Burke grunted, and the two Gardaí moved across to some bright green sofas scattered around the atrium and sat down.

A few minutes later, a man came bustling into the reception area and used his staff card to let himself through the turnstiles. He walked over to where Burke and Moore were seated.

"Good morning, Inspector. My name is Giltrap. I'm John McKenna's manager. What's this I hear about John? He hasn't turned in for work today. Most unusual."

"Is there somewhere a bit more private we can talk, Mr Giltrap?" Burke said.

"Oh, yes, right. There's a meeting room just over here," the man said gesturing to a tiny room off the lobby with four glass walls and a glass door.

When they were seated inside at a small round table, Burke took the initiative.

"What exactly was John McKenna's role here at the bank, Mr Giltrap?"

"Sorry, Inspector, may I ask what all this is about? Is John OK?"

Burke said nothing, so Fiona Moore spoke up.

"I'm sorry to tell you, Mr Giltrap, but John McKenna was killed last night. He was stabbed in a lane downtown and died on his way to hospital."

"Oh, my God. Dear God. That's terrible. Poor lad."

Burke let the information settle on the man who was clearly distressed by the news.

"So, as I was saying, what exactly did Mr McKenna do here at the bank, Mr Giltrap?" Burke asked.

"What? Oh, sorry, I can't quite get my head around it. John, yes, well, he was a member of a team that looks after some of our well-to-do clients. We call it wealth management. He has only – sorry, had – only been with us for three years, but he had a good degree, and was very bright, and the clients liked him a lot too. He was set for great things here at the National, let me tell you."

"And who would these clients of his have been, in the main?" Burke said.

"I'm sorry, Inspector, but we have very strict confidentiality rules here, you know. I couldn't possibly divulge that kind of information."

Moore braced herself.

"I see. So, what you are saying is that if I want to find out anything more about John McKenna's work, I'll have to get a warrant and then come back with a team of, say, thirty uniformed officers and seize his computer and all his files, as well as God knows what else. Won't look too good in front of all your other staff, not to mention your well-to-do clients, Mr Giltrap."

Edmund Giltrap remained silent as he processed what Burke had just said.

"Look, Inspector, I can tell you a little about John's work, but I can't name names. OK?"

"Go on."

"John had a portfolio of just twelve clients. Next year, we would have given him another handful, as he got more used to dealing with them. His job was to analyse their investments and suggest how better to leverage their wealth to make more money. He had a range of the bank's products at his disposal, and he could go outside the bank on a brokerage basis if needs be to get particular investment plans if his clients required."

"What sort of amounts was he dealing with, Mr Giltrap?" Moore asked.

"I'm really not comfortable discussing this, Sergeant. It's very private business."

"Oh, go on. No names, remember? And we just need approximate amounts – not euros and cents," Moore said, leaning in a little closer to the banker.

"Well, he would have had something in the order of six billion under management, although it would vary depending on exchange rates and interest rates at any time," Giltrap said.

"Wow! Quite a sum. And would many of these clients be Irish?" Burke said.

"No. Only one is Irish. God, I'll have to pass his portfolio over to Declan. The clients hate that. We like to provide continuity for them, and they expect it."

"And where would the other eleven clients come from?" Moore asked. She felt she was getting the recalcitrant banker to open up a bit.

"They are international – from all over. I don't have their locations memorized, I'm afraid."

Burke knew the man was lying, but he let the lie pass for the moment.

"But you can't think that his– his death, I mean, can be in any way connected to his work here?" Giltrap said.

"Could be – maybe not. It's very early days, but we may need to look at some of his stuff in any case. Did John have any close friends in the bank?" Burke said.

"Oh, yes. He was very popular. He often went out with his workmates in the evening or at the weekend, and I think he may have been seeing a girl from the mortgage department too. We have to be careful with that kind of thing for security reasons, you know."

"We'll need to have her name and contact details, Mr Giltrap, and a list of his friends here. Can you arrange that?" Burke said.

"Well, I suppose so, but it's a bit irregular."

"So is murder," Burke said.

The banker shuddered slightly, but didn't respond.

"Right. Well, that's all for the moment, Mr Giltrap. Here's my card. My email address is on it so you can send me the details for John's girlfriend and associates. I presume that will be later today?" Moore said.

"Well, I'll need to consult HR, but yes, I suppose so."

"Thanks for your time. We'll be in touch."

* * *

When Giltrap got back to his office on the fourth floor, he called Declan Nevin in and the two of them went to another one of the little glass-walled meeting rooms.

Giltrap told Nevin what had happened to his colleague. Declan Nevin took a moment to digest the news, and then composed himself.

"I want you to take over his clients, Declan. Don't tell them what has happened to John, obviously, just say he's away for a while. Have a good trawl through the accounts too. See if they're all in good order, and then you had better call Internal Audit in and ask them to go over them. But come back to me first if you find anything odd, OK?"

"Yes, sure. You don't think there's any connection to his work, do you?" Nevin said.

"Hardly, but we need to be sure everything is shipshape. I don't want any surprises with the police sniffing around. Oh, and what's the name of that girl John was going out with in Mortgages? I suppose I'd better tell her what's happened. I'm not looking forward to that one!"

"Emma, Emma Rowe. Shall I ask her to come up?"

"I guess. Better to get it over with. Let's see if I have a clean hanky."

Emma Rowe was summoned from the depths of the open plan offices and informed that Mr Giltrap wanted to see her. She was immediately nervous, thinking that she must have made some dreadful error that would cost the bank a fortune, so she made her way upstairs with all sorts of wild imaginings going through her head. She found Giltrap who was by now back at his cubicle, and introduced herself rather tentatively.

"Miss Rowe – sorry, Emma, come with me, we need to have a little chat," Giltrap said.

Giltrap's introduction did nothing to calm her nerves. She was sure she was in for the chop, though she couldn't for the life of her think why.

When they were seated in the same small, glass-walled meeting room where Giltrap had spoken to Declan Nevin, he broke the news of John McKenna's death to the girl. She immediately dissolved into uncontrollable sobbing, and Giltrap didn't know how to respond. He was mortally embarrassed.

"Would you like a glass of water, Emma?" he said, in as sympathetic a voice as he could manage.

Emma Rowe shook her head, still looking down at the table and clutching Giltrap's handkerchief which he had donated a few moments earlier. The sobbing continued.

"Perhaps I'll get one of the girls from HR to come and be with you," he said, not knowing what else to do. He made an internal call, and was relieved to find that there was someone available.

"Just before you go, Emma, did John say anything to you about his work? Anything that could give us a clue as to what might have happened to him?"

"No, of course not," Emma said, pleased to be a little bit distracted from the embarrassing silence. "We never really spoke about work – just some of the people here, that's all. We've been going out for over a year. We were going to get engaged."

The sobbing started anew.

Chapter Five

"What did you make of that?" Burke said as they crawled back through the traffic towards Store Street Garda station.

"Hard to tell. He's a typical banker – keeps things close to his chest. But I'd say it has put the wind up him a bit. When we get back, I'll have a root around and see if there's anything on the bank that looks a bit off. What do we do now?" Moore said.

"Fuck knows. Let's see if forensics got anything at the scene. Then I want to start on his mates. We'll need to get back to the family and lift his computer. See what sort of thing he's into on social media – all that stuff. Did they find his mobile phone?"

"I don't know, but I'll follow it up."

When they got back to the station, Burke parked up in the yard at the back of the building.

"You go on in, I'll be back in a few minutes," Burke said.

"Right, boss."

Fiona Moore had a good idea where her colleague was going, but she knew better than to ask.

Burke walked across the road to Nesbitt's pub. As soon as the barman saw him come in, he put on a pint of Guinness and poured a small Irish whiskey. Burke waited patiently for the Guinness to settle, and then the barman topped it off.

"Grand day, Aidan," the barman said.

"Is it now? A grand day to be stabbed and left dying in a lane is what it is."

"Oh, yeah. I heard about that – poor bugger. Have you got anyone yet for it?"

"Jesus, give us a chance, will ye, Danny. What's the crack anyway?"

"Ah, ye know, same old same old."

"Hmmph."

Burke downed his pint in one go, and followed it up quickly with the whiskey chaser. He threw a ten euro note on the counter and eased himself off the bar stool.

"See ya later, Danny," he said.

* * *

Back in the station, Burke sat at his desk thinking. Murders in the city were usually associated with either the drugs trade, or some struggle for territory among the few gangs that demented the local Gardaí with their nonsense, or sometimes, a combination of both. But this one didn't seem to fit the pattern. He felt that John McKenna was neither a member of a gang, nor was he in any obvious way connected to the drugs trade, although Burke knew that in some quarters, well-off business types could occasionally be caught up in cocaine use. But it didn't usually end in death.

He got up, and collected Fiona Moore again.

"C'mon, Fiona, let's go and see the McKennas. Have a poke around this fella's room. See what we can find."

* * *

As lunchtime approached, the McKenna household had become a busy place. Pat McKenna's sister had arrived having learned of the tragic news first thing that morning. Neighbours were coming and going, and a constant supply of tea, sandwiches and cake was being manufactured by the woman from the house next door. The sense of community in these parts of Dublin was still very strong, and in dark days such as this, everyone rallied round to do what they could to support the unfortunate family.

The door to the modest house was open when Burke and Moore pulled up in the brightly coloured squad car. They made their way inside, and as soon as Pat McKenna spotted them, he came over.

"Inspector. What can we do for you this morning?" he said.

Burke introduced Moore to the man, and said, "We were wondering if we could take a look at John's bedroom, Mr McKenna? Sorry to barge in, but time is of the essence in these cases."

"John's not in any hurry anymore," McKenna said wistfully, "but I suppose that would be OK. It's at the top of the stairs on the right of the landing. Go on up. But don't make a mess, will you? Mary wouldn't like that."

"No, of course not. Do you know if John had a computer, Mr McKenna?" Moore said.

"Aye, he did. He got it last year with the money from his bonus. It should be up there on the dresser."

Burke and Moore climbed the steep stairs to the landing and went into John McKenna's bedroom.

Unlike the rest of the house, which looked as if it hadn't been re-decorated since the 1950s, John's bedroom was modern. The walls were painted a neutral mid-grey colour, and the furniture looked as if it had recently come from Ikea. It was neat, functional and quite new. The dresser the lad's father had referred to was more like a small desk with a lamp, a stack of three bright yellow stationery trays, and a small inkjet printer. The laptop was on top of the desk, still connected to the mains, but switched off.

Moore donned vinyl gloves and did a quick search around the single bed, looking inside the pillowcases, underneath the mattress and under the bed itself. She searched the drawer of the small nightstand, and his wardrobe where three or four outfits hung neatly on hangers, but found nothing of any significance.

Burke had by this time opened the laptop and switched it on, which was about as far as his technical capabilities stretched.

"Here, Fiona, can you get any sense out of this thing?"

Moore came across and saw that the machine was password-protected.

"I don't want to start messing with it in case it locks us out permanently. Let's get it back to the station and give it to the techies to play with. They'll get into it quick enough," Moore said.

"Right. Bring the power cable too. I'm going to have a quick shuftie in his papers."

Burke thumbed his way down through the small pile of A4 pages that had been stored in the yellow trays. It was all very normal. Letters to one or two utilities complaining about this and that. A renewal notice for insurance on the house. A few tax forms from the Revenue Commissioners and a birthday card in the form of a cartoon with Superman on the front carrying the message, 'All my love to my superhero – Emma xxxx'.

They took the laptop back downstairs and sought out Pat McKenna again.

"Mr McKenna, we need to take John's PC back to the Garda station if that's OK? We'll mind it carefully, but it may contain some information that could be of use to us," Burke said.

"Take it. It's no use to him now, and I know nothing about those things anyway."

"And, Mr McKenna, we'd like to get a list of John's friends from you at some stage. Do you think we could come back later when things are a bit quieter?" Moore asked.

"Why don't I drop down to Store Street when these people have gone. I could do with the walk and getting out for a bit, to be honest. I'll come down around six."

"Six. Yes, that would be fine. Thanks. See you later."

* * *

The Garda Technical Bureau is based in the Phoenix Park where An Garda Síochána have their headquarters. The unit is comprised of a mixture of members of the force, and civilian workers with specialist expertise in various areas. In recent years, the bureau has established a number of specialities in information technology. They are viewed as a different species by the rank-and-file Gardaí, but they have developed very advanced skills, often working closely with international forces, including Europol, the various UK police forces, and on occasion, even the FBI.

Moore put a call through to them, explaining the situation about John McKenna's laptop.

"We can send someone down to you, if you like?" the officer at the other end of the phone said.

"Could you? That would be great. Who should we expect, and when?"

"Hang on a minute now, I'll see who's free. Let me see." Moore could hear the officer tapping his keyboard. "Here we are, I can get Jane Langford down to you in about an hour. Jane is very good with computers. She'll have it open in no time for you."

"Fantastic. Thanks a lot. Get her to ask for Sergeant Moore at the front desk, and I'll look after her."

When Moore had finished the call with 'The Park' as it was known, she received a call from forensics.

"Hi, Fiona. It's Jim here from the lab. We're just about finished now on the site where your McKenna was done in."

"Right. Did you find anything?" Moore said.

"Well, we found a knife. As we thought, it had been dumped in one of the bins along the lane. Great job that – going through the waste from several restaurants and pubs. You want to see what they throw out."

"Eh… no I don't, actually. What about the weapon anyway?"

"We're working on it now. We need to match the blood on it to McKenna to be sure it is the murder weapon, but it looks like it. There are a few prints on it, but no matches in our database. But there is something odd," Jim said.

"What?"

Moore was aware that forensics often tried to build up to a vital piece of information by creating suspense. She disliked the practice intensely, but put up with it without saying anything. After all, they did have a terrible job.

"There appears to be some sort of Russian writing on the blade where you would expect to see the maker's name. At least, that's what one of the guys here says it is – apparently, he studied Russian in college."

"Can he translate it?"

"It's not translatable. Just seems to be a maker's name written in Cyrillic letters. A and R Zlatoust. Seems they make a lot of hunting knives and stuff."

"Can you buy them here?" Moore said.

"Dunno. That's your job, Detective. We're just humble forensic scientists."

"OK, thanks Jim. Let me know when you have confirmation of the blood, won't you?"

"Yes, sure. See ya."

Chapter Six

Emma Rowe shared an apartment with two other girls on the south side of the River Liffey near Grand Canal Dock. It was a good location, taking just fifteen minutes to walk to work, with a great array of bistros, bars, and restaurants nearby. Emma had her own room in the apartment, the other two girls sharing the second bedroom, which meant that she paid half of the rent. But she could afford it, and in any case, it wasn't a permanent arrangement as she would be getting somewhere with John quite soon. Well, that had been the plan.

She arrived home shortly after six o'clock, not being in any humour to go out after work with any of her colleagues. It was getting dark, with rain due, but Emma had managed to stay dry on the walk home. She'd have to tell her parents about John's death this evening. They lived in Waterford, about one hundred miles from Dublin. She had brought John home on two or three occasions, but her parents had never really taken to him. It was one of those situations where they felt he wasn't good enough for her, being their only daughter, and while nothing was said overtly, she knew from their behaviour that this was the case.

"No one would be good enough," she had said to John, trying to reassure him when it became clear that he did not have their complete approval.

Her parents would of course be sympathetic, but they would also quite possibly be somewhat relieved at the young man's passing, expecting that their only daughter would ultimately do much better for herself. She wasn't looking forward to making the call.

* * *

Emma went into her bedroom to change out of her work clothes. As she closed the door, a man sprang from where he had been hiding behind the door and grabbed her. He encircled her waist with his left arm, and put his right hand over her mouth to stop her crying out.

"I've done your boyfriend, now it's your turn, you sad bitch," he growled in her ear.

It took Emma a second or two to realise what was happening, but she wasn't one to give in easily. She stamped down hoping to connect with the arch of the man's foot, and she wriggled furiously. She managed to sink her teeth into his right hand, and although he was wearing gloves, her teeth were sharp, and quickly drew blood, causing him to yelp in pain.

Her foot connected with his left trainer too. Still wearing her stout work shoes, and stamping furiously, she broke several of the man's bones, causing him to cry out again, and temporarily release his grip on her.

Free from his grasp, Emma lunged forward to her dressing table where her hair dryer was lying. She grabbed it, and with as much force as she could muster, spun around and whacked her assailant across the face as he advanced on her again. The blow hit home. The sharp end of the hair dryer caught his left eye, bruising his temple and causing him to lose his vision as his eye filled with blood. He bent forward clutching his face, blood pouring from the wound and dripping onto Emma's bed.

Emma decided that flight was preferable to fight. She had been lucky so far, but he was quite a big man, and if he got hold of her again, it could be curtains for her. She jumped over his legs, and ran screaming from her apartment, down the stairs and out onto the street. There were a number of passers-by making their way home through the light evening rain, and Emma readily found a helpful girl with a mobile phone. She dialled 999 and asked for the police.

* * *

Fiona Moore overheard the shout on the Garda radio that was sitting on a desk close to where she was finishing up for the day. She recognised the name of the victim from earlier, so she noted the address and took off. There was no sign of Burke anywhere, so she resolved to call him as soon as she got into her car.

Burke didn't hear his phone. It was buried in his inside jacket pocket, and the din in the busy pub drowned out the tune it was playing. He set about his third pint, sat back and relaxed.

When Moore got to Emma Rowe's address there were two white Garda cars outside, still with their blue lights flashing. A female officer was standing at the entrance to the apartments, so Moore introduced herself.

"Hi, Guard. What happened here?" Moore said.

"Hello, Sergeant. A girl was attacked in her apartment upstairs. She managed to get free, and raise the alarm. We were here in under three minutes, but whoever it was had fled. He left a good deal of his blood behind though."

"Right. Where's the girl?"

"She's back up there with one of our lads giving him the details."

"OK. I'll go on up so."

When Moore got to the apartment, Emma Rowe was talking to one of the uniformed Gardaí, seated at the kitchen table. Moore took a seat at the remaining chair, and listened as Emma recounted her ordeal. It struck Moore that the girl was very composed, given what she had just been through. When she had finished relating her story, Moore said, "God, Emma. That was nasty. Have you any idea what it was all about? Did you get a good look at the guy?"

"No, I'm afraid not. He was behind me most of the time until I whacked him with the hair dryer, and then he covered up his face. I've given what description I could to Tony here," she said, nodding in the direction of the uniformed officer.

"Right. Well, listen, I don't think you should stay here tonight. We need to do a forensic sweep of the place, and in any case, you might not be safe. Is there anywhere you could go?"

"I can't think of anywhere. I'm not from Dublin, and apart from the two girls I share with, I don't really know anyone well enough to impose. Oh, God, what will they do? Do they have to move out too?"

"It's probably best. Why don't you all book into the hotel on Grand Canal Dock? It will only be for a night or two, and I'll make sure they give you a good rate."

"That's a good idea. Can I get some things from the bedroom? Would that be OK?"

"Yes, fine. But don't disturb the bedding, and be careful not to walk in the blood on the carpet. We may be able to get some ID from that. I'll call out the forensics now. Can you contact your flatmates and tell them to go to the hotel?"

"Yes, no problem. I'll call Irene now."

Moore went out onto the landing and made several phone calls. She requested a forensics team to attend the apartment block, then she tried Burke again, and this time managed to get through to him. She told him what had happened, and said she was happy to handle it as he wasn't available. They agreed to leave it to Moore for this evening and to meet in the morning for an update.

The uniformed Gardaí organised a search of the surroundings, but came up with nothing. The intruder had got clean away, though he was probably quite badly injured, so Moore told them to put the hospitals on the alert for someone coming in with an eye injury.

With the forensic team en route, Moore left the uniformed Gardaí in place and drove Emma around to the hotel to book her in. When they were in Moore's car, she asked, "What's all this about, Emma?"

"How do you mean?"

"Well, it's obvious there's something going on here, what with John's murder, and now this. Either you have some very nasty friends, or you've managed to upset someone pretty badly. Why don't you tell me about it?"

"I don't know what you mean. There's nothing 'going on' as you suggest. We were just a young couple working in the same bank going out with each other, and going to get engaged."

Emma Rowe started crying again, holding her hand to her face to try and disguise her tears.

"We will get to the bottom of it, you know. Whatever it is. It would be best if you told us about it before we have to find out for ourselves," Moore said.

"There's nothing to tell. Now leave me alone."

* * *

When Moore had sorted out the accommodation at the hotel, and as promised, secured a very reasonable room rate for Emma and her two flatmates, she drove back around to Emma's apartment.

She was pleased to see the forensic team's large white 4x4 parked outside. Inside, three people in scene-of-crime suits were working away busily, looking for traces of the attacker. Some of his blood had been recovered from the floor, and it would be sent away for DNA profiling. With any luck, they might have information on the perpetrator on file.

Moore spoke to Peter Byrne whom she knew as the forensic lead for this team.

"Hi, Peter. Nasty one this, eh?"

"Yeah, I guess. But wasn't she some feisty little minx that managed to deal with him though? By the sound of it, he may well have intended to kill her."

"Hmm… you're right, I guess. But for the life of me I can't figure out why. How did he gain entry to the apartment?"

"That's the odd thing. No sign of forced entry, and there are good stout locks on the front door. The windows are all secured from the inside, and anyway, there's a sheer drop to the ground thirty metres below. It's almost as if someone let him in, or maybe he even had a key."

"Could the lock have been picked?" Moore said.

"I don't think so, not without some very sophisticated electronics. The keys are cut along their length and there are depressions drilled into the shaft as well. Those are a beggar to pick unless you really know what you're doing," Byrne said.

"Any prints anywhere?"

"Loads. But I doubt if any belong to the intruder. I think Emma told Tony he was wearing gloves."

"Yeah, but she bit his hand through the glove, so he may have removed it as he fled. Have a good look around outside on the landing and the downstairs door handle too, we might just get lucky."

"Righto, Sarge."

When Moore got back outside she spoke to the uniformed Garda at the door.

"Any sign of yer man?"

"No, Sergeant. The lads have had a good look round and two of the cars went off to comb the streets nearby, but no trace so far anyway."

"Hmm, OK. Thanks."

Fiona Moore tried to put herself into the mind of the assailant. Where would he go to get patched up? What would his next move be? He could hardly turn up to the accident and emergency department in a hospital. Those places always had a few Gardaí hanging around at night, and those are the last people he would want to encounter. There were a few privately run medical centres around the city, often attached to pharmacy shops, but these usually closed up at six, or even earlier, so they wouldn't be any use to him. Maybe he was sufficiently well-connected to have his own doctor available. She just didn't have enough information to be useful, so she resolved to go back to the station and spend some time researching wealth management at the National Bank for herself.

Chapter Seven

Anthony James O'Dowd, known in his circle of undesirable acquaintances as 'Anto', had managed to get clean away from Emma Rowe's apartment without being followed. He was quite badly hurt but he stopped in the entrance to one of the shiny glass and aluminium buildings at the back of the river and sat down on the concrete step where passers-by would assume he was just another homeless man settling down for the evening. He pulled a dirty, creased handkerchief from his jeans pocket and pressed it hard against his wounded face. It was seriously sore, but after about ten minutes, nature performed its miracle and the bleeding stopped. He still couldn't see properly. His vision was blurred, and his good eye was streaming with tears.

After a while, although the bleeding had stopped, he knew things weren't right. He needed medical attention, but of course he couldn't go to a hospital. He got himself up, and covering his face as best he could, keeping to the back streets, he made his way to Dame Street, where there was an all-night pharmacy with a doctor available.

As soon as he entered the premises, the girl behind the counter, seeing the state O'Dowd was in, knew what to do.

She showed him into the tiny room at the end of the counter, and called for her colleague. The doctor entered the cubicle a few moments later. His badge announced him as Dr Khatri, and he sat down in front of O'Dowd and started examining his battered face.

"How did this happen to you?" the doctor said.

"I was in a bleedin' fight, wasn't I?" O'Dowd said.

Dr Khatri said nothing, but continued to examine the damaged man. After a moment, he sat back and addressed the patient.

"I'm fairly certain that you have a fractured bone in your face. You need to go to a proper hospital and get an x-ray. I think St James's is on duty tonight. You can get a taxi outside on the street to take you up there. I'll put some closure straps on the wound itself to ensure it doesn't start bleeding again, but you should go there directly. It's very swollen too. Can you see all right?"

"Kinda. What happens if I don't go to the hospital?" O'Dowd asked.

"That would be very unwise. The bone will heal, but you will suffer permanent damage, and your sight may be badly affected for evermore."

"Right. Thanks, Doc. Just put the strappy things on then, and I'll be off."

Dr Khatri applied two closure plasters across the open wound to Anto's face, and gave the whole area a good wipe with antiseptic swabs.

"OK, you're done. Now off you go to the hospital."

Dr Khatri knew better than to ask the man for money. He dealt with five or more similar cases every night in the little consulting room attached to the pharmacy, and the best they could hope for would be that their patients would buy some painkillers on the way out.

When O'Dowd got outside again, he went around the back of the pharmacy into a narrow lane that was used to service the shops and restaurants on Dame Street. At this time of night it was deserted. He pulled out his mobile phone and dialled. The phone was answered promptly.

"It's me, Anto. I need me money."

"Have you completed the second part of the job?" the man at the other end said.

"No. The bitch attacked me and broke my head. I'm wrecked. But I need me money."

"Sorry, Anto. It was a package deal. You get the whole job done, you get the money. There's nothing for half a job."

"That's not right. I did the fella like you said, that McKenna dude. You owe me two fifty for that at least."

The line had gone dead.

"Fuck it! The bastard."

O'Dowd needed to get his hands on some readies. He was still in the busiest part of the city, so he thought he'd put a scam that he had used a few times previously into action. It was a bit risky, but to hell with it. He had to do something.

He walked back along Dame Street to the bottom of Grafton Street and loitered up against the wall. On the other side of the narrow pedestrianised street, there were two ATMs that saw very frequent use, especially at this time of the evening. O'Dowd waited till a rather elderly man with shopping bags and on his own approached the wall of the bank and started putting his card into the slot, slowly and deliberately pressing the keys on the keypad. O'Dowd was now standing behind the old chap, as if he was in the queue to use the machine next. The machine beeped and whirred, and after a few moments, two nice crisp fifty euro notes and a twenty euro note appeared in the cash slot. O'Dowd pushed forward, slamming the old man into the wall, reached around him, and helped himself to the money. The old man staggered and dropped his shopping, and by the time he had recovered his composure, O'Dowd was away along with his money.

"Thanks grandad!" O'Dowd said as he sprinted away, the pain in his broken foot suppressed by the adrenalin of the mugging, into the shady lanes that he knew so well.

Keeping to the back streets and dark alleys that weave their way behind the main thoroughfares of the city, O'Dowd started heading down to the river. He made his way through the cobbled streets of Temple Bar and crossed the Liffey by the Ha'penny Bridge, mingling easily with the crowds of tourists. Once on the north side of the quays, he weaved an indirect path along Liffey Street, into Middle Abbey Street, then cutting through the multi-story car park, into Prince's Street and across O'Connell Street, only to disappear once again into the narrow lanes.

That's one of the things O'Dowd liked about his native city. You could get from one side to the other in less than forty minutes on foot. In another fifteen minutes, O'Dowd was at the back of the Point Depot, an old warehouse that had been converted into a concert hall. Fifteen minutes more, and he arrived at the holding area for the ferry that would sail in another hour for Holyhead.

O'Dowd dodged around between the vehicles all arranged in numbered lanes, and waited for his chance. Sure enough, after a few minutes, a large white panel van pulled in at the back of the queue, and the driver got out to fetch a hot drink from the kiosk a few metres away that had been set up in the car park, leaving his van open. O'Dowd slithered in through the rear door of the van silently, and pulled it closed behind him. He found himself surrounded by a large number of cardboard boxes of different sizes, each bearing a label from a well-known courier company.

"Excellent," he said to himself, "this will do me nicely," and he settled down hidden from view for a badly needed sleep.

Chapter Eight

The following morning Burke arrived in looking a bit rough and smelling faintly of stale beer. He hadn't shaved, and his shirt was creased, all of which added to his dishevelled appearance.

"So, what's the story about last night?" he asked Moore when he had equipped himself with a strong black coffee.

Moore told him all that she knew. There had been no luck in finding the man who attacked Emma Rowe, and the uniformed lads had given up looking after a couple of hours as other law and order matters demanded their attention.

"Where's the girl now?" Burke asked.

"I put her in the hotel just near her apartment on the harbour. I'm not sure if she's gone into work this morning though."

"Anything from forensics?"

"No, not yet anyway. But to be honest, I don't think they'll get much unless his DNA is in the system, and we won't know that for a few days."

"Fucking great! C'mon. Let's get outta here."

Moore grabbed her jacket from the back of her chair and followed Burke downstairs to his car. She liked her boss, but was finding it increasingly difficult to tolerate his constant drinking and dreadful hangovers that, she felt, were getting in the way of his work.

"Where are we going, boss?"

"You'll see," Burke said.

"It's going to be another one of those days," Moore said to herself as Burke sped off through the morning traffic.

They pulled up outside the National Bank and left the car on double yellow lines. Moore just had time to put the Garda notice in the windscreen and catch up to Burke as he strode purposefully into the reception area.

The same unfortunate girl was on the desk and recognised the visitors immediately.

"Good morning, Inspector. And what can we do for you this morning?" she said, rather too cheerily.

"Giltrap."

The receptionist dialled an internal number on her phone, spoke to someone, and then replaced the receiver.

"I'm afraid Mr Giltrap is in a meeting at the moment, Inspector. Maybe if you could make an appointment?"

Burke said nothing, and walked back towards the main door, as if to leave. But instead of going outside, he raised his elbow and smashed the glass on the little red fire alarm box that was positioned adjacent to the entrance. He walked back to the receptionist amid the cacophony of noise now resounding throughout the building.

"Not any more, he's not," Burke said smiling.

The building began to empty out quickly. Employees came from all sides and exited onto the footpath through the turnstiles that had now automatically sprung open. Some staff members wearing yellow high-vis vests with 'Fire Marshal' on their backs appeared carrying clipboards and attempting to herd the throng into groups so that they could be accounted for.

Burke spotted Giltrap shuffling along in the melee, and approached him.

"Mr Giltrap, we need a word."

"Oh, hello, Inspector. Now is not a very good time, I'm afraid."

"Ah, don't worry. I think you'll find it's a false alarm. Could we go somewhere a bit quieter?"

"Eh, well, OK. I'll just tell the marshal that I'm out safely. Hold on."

Giltrap went off and checked in with one of the yellow-vested employees, and returned to where Burke and Moore were standing to the side of the atrium, so as not to get in the way of the departing staff.

"Right. There's a coffee shop around the corner. Let's go there." Giltrap said.

When they were seated in the cramped quarters of the rather noisy coffee shop, Edmund Giltrap asked what the Gardaí wanted.

"Has Emma Rowe been in touch at all this morning, Mr Giltrap?" Burke asked.

Giltrap shuffled uneasily in his seat, trying to avoid eye contact.

"Well?" Moore prompted.

"Yes. Yes, she has in fact. She told me about the incident last night at her apartment. I have given her a week off. I think she's going home to stay with her parents. Probably just as well."

"Why do you say that?" Burke said.

"Well. You know. Obviously, there will have to be an internal investigation at the bank. It's too much of a coincidence."

"How do you mean?" Moore went on, acting dumb.

"Well, what with what happened to John McKenna, and as we know he was seeing Miss Rowe, so it seems logical to me that as she was attacked too, there must be some kind of connection, and like as not, it concerns work."

"And why would that be, Mr Giltrap? I mean, did their work have anything in common? I thought Miss Rowe was in mortgages and McKenna was in wealth something or other," Burke said.

"That's what we'll have to look into. You are right. There doesn't appear to be any overlap. It's a puzzle."

"It could just be that McKenna shared some information with his girlfriend that is important to someone. Information that they don't want to get out. Is that possible?" Burke said.

Giltrap looked down at the floor again.

"I can't imagine what."

"So, when will the bank's investigation get underway?" Moore said.

"Not for a week or two yet. Internal audit are always very busy, and they have a schedule that they arrange weeks in advance. They have to do that to be fair to the departments they are inspecting. But we could perhaps get them to bump this one up the priority list a bit. It's obviously a very unusual situation," Giltrap said.

"All right. But before any of that, could I ask you to get me details of all the accounts that John McKenna held at the bank, and the same for Emma Rowe?" Burke said.

"I'm not sure if we can do that. We have to observe the Data Protection Act, Inspector."

"Look, Giltrap. As you may have already deduced, I'm not a very conventional cop. I do what I have to do to get results, and I don't give a flying fuck for your data protection whatsit. Furthermore, I don't take kindly to anyone that gets in the way of my investigation. Do you understand?"

"But I can't just break all the rules—"

Fiona Moore cut across the man.

"Mr Giltrap, under the current Data Protection Act, once a data subject has passed away, all protection that they enjoyed whilst alive ceases. So you have no need to worry about John McKenna's data, none at all. As for Emma Rowe's accounts, that information could legitimately be deemed to be connected to John McKenna too."

"Very well, I'll see what I can do," Giltrap said.

"Excellent. I'll send someone round at about five this evening to collect it, OK?" Burke said.

Giltrap didn't reply, but his silence implied consent. After a few moments of awkwardness, Burke drained his cup.

"Right. We're done here, for the moment at least. You should be able to get back into your office by now," Burke said, smiling mischievously.

* * *

Emma Rowe was scared. After Mr Giltrap had telephoned her, she called her parents in Waterford and arranged for her father to collect her from the railway station at two forty-five when the Dublin train arrived.

"Maybe if I get away for a while, all this will die down. Better not to be in Dublin for now, anyway," she said to herself as she packed the few meagre belongings she had taken with her to the hotel. "God, I hope they don't find out."

Chapter Nine

"Did old man McKenna come in last night with a list of his son's friends?" Burke said as they drove back to the station.

"Yeah, he did. But it was just all kicking off with the Rowe girl, so I asked Dónal to talk to him. I'm sure he got the details," Moore said.

"Right. Well when we get back, will you start on the list. I want each of them interviewed. See what we can find out about Mr John McKenna. And I want to know what he was doing in that laneway as well. Seems odd to me. Can you organize that?"

"Yeah, sure. Oh, by the way, that girl Jane from the Technical Bureau didn't make it in yesterday. She called to say she'd been delayed, but she'll be down this morning. I'll get her working on McKenna's computer. What are you getting up to?" Moore asked.

"I have to go out for a while, but I'll be back by lunchtime, or soon after. I'll drop you outside and carry on."

"OK, thanks."

When Moore got back to her desk, Jane, the girl from the Technical Bureau was working beside Detective Garda

Dónal Lawlor in the open plan office. He introduced the girl to Moore.

"Hi, Jane. Have you managed to break into it yet?" she said, looking down at the little black Dell laptop that was on the desk.

"Oh yes. Piece of cake, really. He used his birth date as a password. It was the third thing I tried," Jane said.

Moore wondered if Jane was rubbing it in a bit, but decided to give her the benefit of the doubt.

"OK. Well, let me know what you can get from it. You know what we're after – contacts, emails, social media stuff – all the usual. Dónal, can I have a word?"

Moore and Lawlor went into Burke's office at the end of the corridor. The room was, like Burke himself, a bit dishevelled with various files and papers scattered on the desk and several rather shabby garments weighing down the coat stand on the corner by the window, some of them none too fresh.

"Dónal, did Mr McKenna give you a list of his son's friends and acquaintances last night?"

"Yes, he did. Not many names on it, mind you. He said his best mate was a lad called Terry Devane. He'd been friends with him since they were in school where they were more or less inseparable. There are about four or five more as well, and he mentioned a Fintan and a Tom that work at the bank."

"OK. Well, can you get on and arrange interviews with them all. Try and focus on what McKenna might have told them, or what they knew about his work. And see if you can find out what he was doing out on his own the night he was killed. I doubt if that lane where we found him was one of his normal haunts – but you never know."

"OK, Sarge. Where's the boss?" Lawlor said.

"I'm not sure, to be honest. He was a bit grumpy, so I didn't like to ask," Moore said.

"Nothing new there, then."

"Yes, well never mind that. Let's get on," Moore said.

When Lawlor had left the room, Moore sat in behind her boss's desk. She started tidying up the papers and files – she couldn't help herself – tidiness was part of her nature. As she collected things up into small piles, a sheet of paper fell to the floor. Moore bent down to pick it up, and stopped dead in her tracks. The page was an application form for retirement from the force, and Aidan Burke had filled in the top half, but hadn't completed it.

Moore could see from the form that Burke was just forty-nine years old, which surprised her. He looked a good deal older. Although Gardaí can apply for retirement once they have completed thirty years of service and reached the age of fifty, it's quite unusual for them to do so. In fact, many serving members of the force had been trying to get the government to extend the compulsory retirement age beyond sixty, which was the current limit. Moore was puzzled. Burke had given her no indication that he was thinking of chucking it in, and she felt he might have hinted at such a momentous move – to her at least. She was also a bit miffed that Burke, who was to all intents and purposes her partner, would keep such a thing from her. She put the form away in amongst other papers, and went back out to her own desk.

With the imminent retirement of DI Aidan Burke still playing on her mind, Jane came across and broke into her thoughts.

"Hi. I just thought you might like to know, I've just about finished with McKenna's computer," she said.

"That was quick. Find anything interesting?"

"Potentially, yes. There are a couple of hidden folders on the hard drive. I popped them open, and found various documents and emails relating to some property transactions. It looks as if McKenna owns a few apartments around the city, and at least one of them is in joint ownership with an E. Rowe. Ring any bells?"

"Crikey – yes, it does. That's his girlfriend, Emma. But that's mad. The guy lives at home with his parents. How long has he had these places? Can you tell?"

"I didn't get that far. But hang on, I'll go and get it and we can look at it together."

Jane crossed the room and was back in a couple of moments with John McKenna's laptop.

Jane brought up the files that she had found and showed them to Moore.

"Can you tell what date these come from?" Moore asked.

Jane clicked the mouse and the PC displayed a panel of meta-data about the file.

"There you go – looks like about fourteen months ago for the first one. Then, let me see, yes, here, the last one was just three months ago. That's the one in their joint names," Jane said.

"Any sign of how they are financed?" Moore said.

"Hard to tell from just what's here, but there doesn't appear to be any mortgage portfolio attached to them. However, that could be separate. I can do a bit more digging, but the key to this lies in his bank account. Can you get hold of that?" Jane said.

"I'd say that's one for DI Burke. He has a certain way with him in these matters!"

"I won't ask," Jane said.

"Let me just make a note of the addresses. I'm going to check into these a bit more," Moore said.

* * *

Fiona Moore didn't have to go far to find the first apartment on the list that Jane had retrieved from John McKenna's computer. It was on the fourth floor of a large block behind the IFSC, bordering on what used to be a very rough area till the developers had moved in. Now, it was trendy and chic, and the apartment looked to be in excellent condition.

Moore rang the bell and waited, but there was no response. She rang it again and still no one answered, but it was obvious that the apartment was occupied. She wrote a hasty note with her mobile phone number and name on it, asking the occupier to call her as soon as they got it.

The second apartment was a bit further away on the other side of the river, close to Grand Canal Dock. Again, it was a well-appointed modern block, and this time Moore found the unit on the first floor. Here she had more luck. A moment after ringing the bell, the door was opened by a pretty, slim, blonde girl wearing blue jeans and a pale blue polo shirt.

"Hi. I'm Detective Sergeant Fiona Moore," she said, holding up her warrant card for the girl to inspect. "Could we have a word?"

"Yes, of course. Please, come in." It was clear from the girl's accent that she wasn't a native. Moore guessed that she was probably Eastern European – maybe Polish. She accepted the invitation, and went into the flat.

Inside, the apartment was in immaculate order. It was quite small, but everything was neat and tidy. The furniture was largely from IKEA, but it was tasteful and carefully arranged to make the most of the space, and in very good condition. The living room was an open plan affair with the kitchenette at the end away from the window, and as Moore made her way in, by counting the doors off the narrow hallway, she figured it had just one bedroom.

Once inside, the tenant gestured for Moore to take a seat, and offered her a cup of coffee.

"Thanks, that would be lovely. May I ask your name please?"

"Anya. Anya Piklokov. I'm from Poland, but my papers are all in order."

The girl busied herself preparing the refreshments, but as the room was so small, they could continue their conversation while this was being done.

"Oh, that's fine, Anya, I'm not concerned about that. Do you live here alone?"

"Yes – well, mostly. My boyfriend stays over quite a bit. He's a driver, and when he's not out of town he normally stays with me. Is that OK?"

"Yes, of course. Anya, may I ask if you own the apartment?"

The girl laughed.

"No, of course not. I only work in a bar in the evenings. Tips are good, but not enough to buy a place like this in Dublin."

She brought a mug of strong black coffee over to Moore along with a small jug of milk and a bowl of dark brown sugar.

"Thanks, that's lovely. So, who owns the place then?"

"Mr Patrick. He's very nice. He comes every month to collect the rent. He likes to get cash."

"Do you know his second name, Anya?"

"Yes, of course. He is Patrick McKenna, but we call him Mr Patrick."

"I see. And how old is Mr Patrick?"

"Hmm let me see. A little older than me, I'd say. Maybe twenty-eight. But he could be a bit more. I'm not very good at guessing people's age. I always have to ask for ID at the bar," Anya said smiling.

Moore took out her phone and opened up a photo of John McKenna that she had taken from his driver's license. She showed it to Anya.

"Is this Mr Patrick?"

"Yes, I think so. It's not a good picture, but yes, I think that's him OK. Is he in trouble?"

"We are just making enquiries at the moment, Anya. How long have you lived here?" Moore said.

"I moved in last year. I got a good price because it was without furniture. And Mr Patrick was very helpful. He gave a month's rent free to allow me to buy some stuff.

And I painted the walls in here. There were some marks from the previous people."

"Do you have a lease, or a rent book, Anya?"

"No, nothing like that. Should I have these things? Is that bad?"

"No, it's fine. I was just curious."

Moore tried not to wince as she drank the coffee. It was far too strong for her taste, but she didn't want to cause offense. When she had half of it consumed, she got up and prepared to leave.

"Thanks, Anya, that was lovely. And thank you for being so helpful. You have the place in really nice shape."

"Thank you, Sergeant. You are very different from the police in my country," she said, smiling.

Chapter Ten

Moore got back to the station to find Aidan Burke sitting in his office brooding.

"Come in, Fiona, grab a chair," he said. "So, how are we getting on?"

Moore explained the visit to the apartment and the conversation she had had with the Polish girl.

"Are you sure she said Patrick, not John? Maybe her accent caused confusion," he said.

"No, she was quite clear. Mr Patrick she called him."

"So, do you think it's the father that owns these places, or what?"

"I don't know, boss. But I'd say Emma Rowe might be able to throw some light on it. Pity she's buggered off to Waterford."

"We can easily get her back, if you think it's necessary," Burke said.

"I don't fancy driving all the way down there just to ask her a few questions. And if we call her, she may get spooked and do a runner altogether," Moore said.

"No. That's not what I had in mind. Let's get the local lads to lift her and bring her back here. They'll enjoy a trip to the city, and she'll have lots of time to think about where all this is going on the journey. What do you say?"

"Enough time to make up some right cock and bull story, if you ask me. But I guess we don't have much choice. Shall I arrange it?"

"Yeah. Get her home address from the bank. They should have it under 'next of kin' or something, and then get a couple of Gardaí in a squad car to get her nice and early tomorrow morning and bring her here. Any news on McKenna's friends?"

"I've asked Dónal to arrange interviews with all of them, and to find out why McKenna was on his own in the lane in the wee small hours."

"Good. Let's hope that will tell us something."

"And when I've set up the thing for Emma Rowe, Inspector, we need to talk," Moore said.

Burke looked quizzically at his sergeant, but said nothing. Moore got up and left to make the arrangements.

She was back twenty minutes later.

"All done. Now, let's go across the road. There's something I need to discuss with you," she said.

Burke got up, wondering what all this could be about. He wasn't used to taking orders from his sergeant. They made their way over to Nesbitt's pub. When they went in, Danny reached for a pint glass to start filling it with Burke's favourite tipple, but Moore stopped him.

"That's a pint of lemonade for the Inspector, Danny, and I'll have a coffee please."

They sat down in their usual spot well away from the bar where they could not be overheard. The bar was more or less empty in any case, the lunchtime crowd having returned to their daily grind in the many offices nearby.

"So, when were you going to tell me, Aidan?" Moore asked.

"Tell you what, girl?"

"That you're chucking it in."

Burke said nothing. He wasn't expecting this.

"How did you find out?" he said finally.

"That's not important. But I think you might have had the decency to share it with me. We've been partners for nearly four years now, and we've been through some tough shit. I thought you had more respect for me," Moore said.

"It's not that. I do respect you. I haven't finally decided yet anyway. It's not a done deal. I would have told you sooner or later."

"Yeah, right. At your leaving party, I presume!"

Moore was angry. When Garda officers work closely together over a number of years, they form a bond. It needn't be romantic or sexual, though some do go in that direction, but it's a bond nevertheless. It's essential to keep each other safe when things get rough. That bond doesn't include some private matters that each keeps to themselves, but something like this was not in that domain.

Burke took a swig of his drink, wishing it was black and creamy. He put the glass down.

"Listen, Fiona, can I talk openly with you?"

"I wish you bloody would, Aidan. Don't keep me in the dark, please."

"My life's a mess. Ever since the divorce, I've gone downhill, and I don't like where it's going to end. I'm drinking like a fish, and I don't seem to be able to stop anymore. I'll have to make some major life changes if I'm going to live beyond another five years. My doctor has told me."

"But surely you don't have to chuck in the job?"

"I dunno. All I do know is that I'm not as keen as I used to be. You must see that. It's like I couldn't be arsed anymore. I'm just going through the motions really."

Moore took a moment to digest what Burke had said. She knew she had to tread carefully.

"Look, boss. You're a damn fine cop. Probably one of the best there is. You have more collars to your name than most of us accumulate in a whole career. And you don't shirk from the nasty ones either. Besides, what would you do if you retire? Get a job as a security guard up on the Ballymount Road chasing away rats and scallywags with a dog and a torch at three in the morning? I don't think so."

Burke remained silent, contemplating what Fiona Moore had said.

"Look, I'll help you, if you're up for it. We'll get you sorted. Tear up that form that you left lying around in your office for all to see. What's your house like?"

"How do you mean?"

"I've never been inside. What's it like? Is it cheerful? Bright? Clean and tidy, or scruffy and down at heel?"

"It's a shit-hole."

"Right, well that's the first thing. Get a team of cleaners in and get them to give the place a right good going over. Then, if it's still dull and dreary, get it painted. Then get yourself down to Louis Copeland and buy some new suits and a few shirts. Get some new shoes while you're at it. And maybe a razor?"

"Jesus, girl, you're worse than my bloody wife!"

"You're right, I am – much worse. And I'm going to stay on your case till you get yourself back in the groove, Inspector Aidan Burke. And when we've got you fixed up, then you can decide if you want to desert us or not. OK?"

"Right, OK, OK, don't go on. Now, can I have a bleeding pint of stout?"

"No, you bloody can't! Jeez. Have I been wasting my time or what?"

"All right – keep your knickers on. Let's get back and solve this murder." He left the half-finished glass of lemonade on the table.

Moore had no idea if she had done the right thing. But she did know that things couldn't go on the way they were for much longer.

* * *

Back at the office, Burke spent some time Googling cleaning companies. Moore was right. Living in a pig sty wasn't helping. It didn't take him long to find a company located near to his house in Crumlin, and he called the number to arrange a 'deep clean' for the property for two days hence. He explained that he wanted the place tidied as well, and he instructed the girl on the phone that the team should dump all the old newspapers and other detritus and not to be too fussy – if in doubt, throw it out.

"I'll leave the key under the mat for you," Burke said.

"Eh, we prefer to have the householder on the premises when we do the work, sir. That helps us to avoid any misunderstandings if things can't be found afterwards," the girl said diplomatically.

"Don't worry, there's nothing worth stealing anyway. Just get them to put the key back through the letterbox when they have finished. How much will it cost?"

"That depends on the time spent at your house, sir, but on average, from what you have said, I'd say about one hundred and seventy euro, give or take. Is that OK?"

"Yes, fine."

* * *

Moore felt a bit better after the chat with her boss. He really was a damn good cop, and apart from her personal feelings for the man, it would be a great shame if the force lost such a talent. But he did need to get his life sorted a bit. She just hoped that she hadn't overdone it with him. After all, he was her senior officer.

Feeling that a weight had been lifted, she turned her attention to the case in hand. Moore had a cousin who worked in financial services in the City of London. He was with a merchant bank, but she didn't really understand exactly what his job entailed. Nevertheless, he might be able to fill her in about what goes on in such an establishment.

"Hi, Mark, it's Fiona here from Dublin," she said when she was put through to him.

"Oh, wow, hi Fee. God, I haven't heard from you for a while. Everything OK?"

"Oh, yeah, sure. All good here. Listen, can I pick your brain for a minute. Have you got the time?"

"Yeah, course, though that shouldn't take long!" her cousin said.

"Ha. Look, I'm working on a case here that involves a man who worked in the wealth management part of one of the banks. There's something funny about it though. He seems to have accumulated a pile of money somehow, and I'm wondering if you know of any fiddles that he might have been running."

"It's not the National by any chance?" Mark said.

"Could be, why?"

"Always the policeman, Fee. You never change. It's just they have a bit of a rep here in the City. A lot of our guys won't touch anything of theirs. They deal with a lot of iffy stuff from Eastern Europe. Too dodgy for the likes of us. Anyway, I'd need to know a good bit more about what he was actually dealing in. Can you find out?"

"Probably. Would you be able to tell if we got all the details?" Moore said.

"Well, I don't know, but maybe. I could certainly look into it for you – it's kind of exciting."

"But you must keep it to yourself, Mark. I'm serious now. This is just between you and me, OK?"

"Yes, OK. Let me know what you find out, and I'll see what I can do. Great to hear from you. Are you going to get over here anytime soon? You know there's always a bed for you at ours."

"I doubt it, Mark, but thanks for the offer. I'll call you when I have more. Cheers."

Fiona's cousin Mark was two years younger than she was. The eldest son of her father's brother, James Moore. The two families had grown up close to each other in

County Westmeath, where the farm that belonged to her grandfather had been split between the two boys when he passed on. Houses for each family had been built on the land, and Mark and his sister Eleanor had gone to the same schools as Fiona. The land, being very fertile, was sufficient to support the two families, and both James and Fiona's father were hard working men who exploited it to the full to provide a good living for their dependents. But splitting the farms again for the latest generation would have been inefficient, and in any case none of them were particularly interested in the hard life that farming required, so they had all left the land and gone to jobs in the cities, but kept in fairly close contact all the same.

Chapter Eleven

Moore felt that there might be a bit of coolness between Burke and herself after the chat they had had in the pub earlier, but it wasn't so. Burke was cheery, and seemed to have been encouraged by his sergeant's suggestions, as they made their way to the home of Pat and Mary McKenna.

"Sorry to disturb you again, Mr McKenna," Moore said as Pat McKenna opened the door.

"Oh, it's you. You'd better come in."

Mary and Pat McKenna were in the small sitting room where the television was broadcasting some mindless quiz show. When Mrs McKenna saw who their visitors were, she got up and turned it off promptly.

"Can I get you a cup of tea, officers?" she asked.

"Thanks, that would be lovely," Burke said, nodding to Fiona Moore to accompany the woman to the kitchen. When the two women had left the room, Burke said to McKenna, "Mr McKenna, we have received information that John appears to have been the owner of a number of apartments in the city centre. Do you know anything about that?"

McKenna stared at Burke as if he had suddenly sprouted two heads.

"Are ye mad, or what? That's stuff and nonsense. Sure, if he had apartments, why do you think he'd be living here on top of us? No, you've got that wrong, Inspector."

"I don't think so, Mr McKenna. And the weird thing is, these apartments are in the name of Patrick McKenna – your name."

"Well, now I've heard it all," the man said, a wry smile beginning to form at the edge of his mouth.

"You're joking with me now, aren't you? Tell me, why are you really here today, Inspector?"

"I'm not joking, sir. I promise you our information is good. John owns three apartments in various parts of Docklands, one of them jointly with Emma Rowe, and the other two solely in the name of Patrick McKenna. Are you saying you didn't know anything about this?"

Just then, Mary McKenna re-entered the room carrying a tray with four cups and saucers, a teapot, milk jug, sugar bowl and a plate of sweet sponge cake cut into triangular slices.

"Wait till you hear this, Mary. Mr Burke is only after telling me that John owned three apartments in town. Three, no less, and all in my name. What do you make of that?"

Mary McKenna put the tray down on the occasional table in front of the tiled fireplace, but said nothing.

She took a crumpled tissue from the apron that she had donned in order to prepare the refreshments, and dabbed her nose.

"Well, Mary, did you know anything about this?" McKenna said.

"It's all rubbish, Pat, as you well know. John – a man of property?" She turned to Burke. "What are you doing coming round here with your talk of apartments. Can't you see we're only ordinary people just about getting by on Pat's pension. We're not exactly property moguls now, are we? Although we do own this little place, and that'll do us, won't it, Pat?"

Moore, who had come back into the room behind Mrs McKenna, spoke up, addressing both of them.

"So, you are saying you are not the beneficial owner of any apartments here in town, and furthermore, you were completely unaware of the fact that John had these investments?"

"Correct, miss. But wait – what if there is some truth to what you say, although I don't see how it can be? What will happen to these 'investments' as you call them now that John is dead?" Pat McKenna said.

"That's not for us to say, sir. It depends on a few things, like, did John have a will? And it would have to be established that the ownership of the apartments was totally legitimate, of course. If I may make a suggestion, I think you should consult a solicitor as soon as possible to start sorting it all out," Burke said.

Mrs McKenna poured out the tea, and the four of them sat in silence. No one, it seemed, was in the humour for cake.

* * *

When the detectives had left, Mary and Pat McKenna sat in bewilderment in the tiny front room of their little cottage.

"What do you think, Mary. Is it possible John is in fact the owner of these places? Are you sure he never said anything at all to you that might have given you a hint? He talked more to you than he did to me."

"Jesus, Pat, I had no idea of any of this. Sure, wouldn't I have told you if I had known? And God knows what we're getting into with all of this. Solicitor indeed. We never had anything to do with any solicitor."

"I suppose I could ask Barry down at the corner. He had some dealing with a solicitor a few months back. I don't know if the blighter was any good or not, but it would be no harm to ask in any case. What do you think?"

"Aye, do that, Pat. Now, give me your cup, there's still tea in the pot."

* * *

"What did you make of that?" Fiona Moore said on the way back to the Garda station.

"I think they were being truthful. Maybe the mother knew a bit more than she was letting on, but I doubt if it amounts to much. It doesn't help us any. We need to find the motive for John's stabbing – or maybe it was just a random act of madness. But I'm not convinced. What do you think?"

"I think you're right. I don't think the McKennas were aware of what John was up to. We'll have to give Emma Rowe a good grilling in the morning, see if we can get to the bottom of it."

When they got back, there was a message waiting for Burke saying that the Superintendent wanted to see him.

He made his way to Superintendent Jerome Heffernan's office, knocked and entered when summoned from within.

Heffernan was a Cork man who had come up through the ranks in the southern capital to the point where he could go no further. In order to complete his escalation in the force, he had had to come to Dublin to take up the role as Detective Superintendent, but it didn't sit easy on him. His discomfort was nothing to do with the normal rivalry between the two cities, which was, in any case, largely good-humoured banter. He just didn't feel at home in Dublin, and he travelled back to the place of his roots as often as he could possibly manage. He was a man of much the same age as Aidan Burke, but there the similarities ended.

Heffernan was broad shouldered, trim, with immaculately groomed grey hair and a round ruddy face.

He was a big man, but his clothes fitted well, and he was always beautifully turned out. Naturally, he spoke with a Cork accent, but of the more refined kind that is associated with the better off cohort of Cork's mixed and varied citizens.

"Come in, Aidan, sit down. How's things?" Heffernan said.

"Ah, you know. Up and down. You wanted to see me, sir."

"Yes. I understand you're working on this John McKenna killing. I've had a call from the boss man of the National Bank, Geoffrey McGroarty if memory serves. He's not a happy camper, Aidan, not at all."

"No, well he wouldn't be, would he? One of his employees is dead, and another scared out of her home. It's hardly the best publicity for his organisation now, is it?"

"True. But that's not what he's unhappy about, it seems. He says that you have been leaning on another of his people, a Mr Giltrap. Giltrap has complained to his boss about your methods, and has asked that you don't have any more truck with the man. Is he right?"

"No, sir. Pardon the French, but that's bollocks. There's something rotten in the state of Denmark, as it were, and we need to get to the bottom of it. It may well be connected to the lad's death. To be honest, I'm just getting started on Giltrap."

"I see. I suppose they could be trying to call off the dogs to cover something up. But this is a sensitive area, Aidan. The National has a good number of Government accounts and they have friends in what they consider to be high places. I don't want to be getting a call from Government Buildings over this. That wouldn't do at all. Tell you what. Why don't we say that this conversation took place tomorrow, not today, and that gives you another day to do your worst. But go easy. I'll tell

McGroarty that you're out of the office till tomorrow. OK?"

"Yes, sir, but depending on what I uncover, we may not be able to keep this low profile for long."

"We'll see. I want you to report back to me before you do anything dramatic though. Any sign of the press sniffing around?"

"No. They've moved on from the McKenna thing now. Unfortunately, there's too much crime on our streets to keep them interested in a single stabbing for very long," Burke said.

"That's what we have you for, Aidan. Now go on and see to your banker, but remember what I said."

Burke left the office. The Superintendent's little speech had exactly the opposite effect on him than Heffernan had intended. He was ready to tear Giltrap apart to find out what he was hiding, and he didn't really care if it would be a bad career move. He might not be in the job much longer anyway, despite what he had said to Fiona Moore.

Chapter Twelve

Emma Rowe was horrified to be woken at seven-thirty in the morning to discover that there was a squad car at the door of her parents' house, and that they were going to take her to Dublin to 'help the Gardaí with their enquiries'. She was embarrassed for herself, and even more so for her parents, who were just a regular man and wife with a good reputation in their neighbourhood. Tongues would be wagging for weeks after this.

She got dressed and packed as quickly as she could, and bade her folks goodbye, hoping to keep the brightly coloured Garda car at the door for as short a time as possible.

On the way to Dublin, she attempted to engage the driver and his mate to discover what was going on, but neither had any insight into why they had been asked to chauffeur the woman to the capital.

"I'm sorry, love, we haven't a clue. All we were asked to do was to collect you and bring you to Store Street station. After that, you know as much as we do," the driver said.

"I was attacked in my flat, you know," Emma persisted, trying to rouse their interest enough to tell her a little more about what exactly was taking place, but to no avail. Eventually she sat back and relaxed a little as the car sped towards Dublin.

Burke had arranged for Fiona Moore to interview Emma when she arrived as he wanted to go back to the bank and have another go at Giltrap. When he arrived at the bank, the receptionist looked up and said, "Mr Giltrap, I presume?"

"Yes, please. And I hope he's not in a meeting," Burke said with a mischievous look in his eye.

The girl made an internal phone call, and then said to Burke, "Mr Giltrap will be down directly, sir, if you'd just like to take a seat."

Giltrap appeared and the two men went off to another of the small glass meeting rooms. When they were seated, Giltrap tackled Burke about what he deemed to be harassment.

"You may as well know, Inspector, that I have lodged a complaint with your office about these meetings. That stunt with the fire alarm was well out of order. Someone could have been injured, you know."

"Not as badly injured as John McKenna, Mr Giltrap. And you may as well know that when I come across someone who tries to throw me off the scent of an inquiry, I get even more unpleasant and determined to uncover what's going on. So, you have to decide. Are you going to help us properly with this and tell us all you know, or are you going to continue to prick about and get in the way?"

Giltrap remained silent for a moment as if he was deciding which route to go down. If he told Burke what he had discovered, it could open up a very large can of worms for both the bank and himself. But if he stayed quiet, he had no insight into how unpleasant Burke could actually be in his pursuit of the truth. It wasn't much of a choice.

"Very well, Inspector, I'll level with you. We've had a careful look at the accounts that John McKenna was managing, and we're not entirely happy about what we have found."

"Go on."

"There appears to be a lot of activity on one of his accounts in particular, that we wouldn't expect to see. A lot of buying and selling of unit trusts over a short space of time, that sort of thing."

"And why would you not expect that kind of activity, Mr Giltrap?"

"Well, unit trusts are largely a long-term investment. You don't normally buy and sell them quickly. You see, there's a five percent spread between the buy and sell price, and you need to hold the investment for some time to allow the units to overtake the cost of the transaction."

"I see. And what about the instructions to do these transactions. How are they conveyed to the bank?"

"Normally by fax, or very occasionally, with highly trusted clients, by phone. We do record all phone calls. But we've checked John's paperwork. There are faxes for each of the transactions he carried out."

"Faxes can quite easily be forged – especially plain paper ones. I've seen it before. Have you checked with the source of the instruction for verification?"

"We're doing that at the moment, but it takes quite a while – different time zones and all that."

"Were the clients disadvantaged by these transactions, if they turn out to be dodgy?"

"Not that we can see. Apart from the bid-offer spread, that is, but the money appears to balance out fine. We have to do more work on it to be certain."

"OK, well keep digging and let me know what you find. And I'd like the details of the particular account involved. And there's something else. We've discovered that McKenna appears to own three apartments here in town, but they're held in the name of his father, Pat McKenna, who claims to know nothing about them. We're bringing Emma Rowe in for questioning today over it. Her name is on one of the deeds too along with McKenna's."

"Bloody hell. I didn't know that. God, this is a mess. Look, I'd really appreciate it if we could keep all of this to ourselves until we find out what's going on. If the press got hold of this, it could start a run on the bank."

"They won't hear it from us, Mr Giltrap. If they do get hold of anything, it will be from inside these four walls. Did you get together details of McKenna's accounts here at the bank for us?"

"Yes, I have them upstairs. But I've looked over them. There's nothing untoward that I can see. Just his salary going in, and various direct debits that look perfectly normal. He does appear to have gotten through a good deal of cash, mind you. But that's hardly suspicious as he didn't have to pay rent or fund a mortgage."

"Right. Could you do me a favour? Have a look for accounts in the name of Patrick McKenna too, will you? Anything with the same address as John's. I'll send someone to collect it all later, if that's OK?" Burke said.

"Yes, all right. But this is a bit unconventional, Inspector. Data protection and all that."

"So is murder, Mr Giltrap; so is murder."

* * *

At this time of day, Burke would usually stop by Nesbitt's on the way back to the station and down a couple of pints of Guinness and a glass or two of Jameson's Irish whiskey. But not today. Today, he diverted himself to Exchequer Street to the premises of Louis Copeland who was well known for his excellent tailoring. There he was measured, and tried on two suits. One was a mid-grey number with a single vent to the back of the jacket, traditionally cut with straight trousers and no turnups. The other was a dashing navy pinstripe, more fitting for a city gent than a rough and tumble Detective Garda. But he ordered them both all the same, and selected three white shirts in good quality cotton and two ties to go with the outfits. The suits, which needed the waistband to be let out a little to accommodate Burke's girth, would be done in three days, and he left the rest of his purchases behind until everything was ready.

"Jesus, look at me," he said to himself when walking back. "That bloody woman has got to me already. What am I like?"

* * *

Emma Rowe was very unhappy. She had spent the journey from Waterford to Dublin contemplating her situation. She knew she hadn't done anything that was out and out criminal, but she had facilitated John McKenna's activity at the bank, and she wasn't sure what sanctions might await her as a result.

She had prepared what she thought would be a convincing story in her own head whilst seated in the back of the Garda car, and she hoped that whoever was going to question her would be satisfied with that.

When she arrived at Store Street, the driver from Waterford handed her over to the desk sergeant, and she was escorted to an interview room at the far end of the building. The room was small, but neat and tidy, and by the looks of it quite recently decorated. There was a large window looking out onto the courtyard at the back of the station, but Emma noticed that it only opened enough to allow some ventilation – escape by that means was out of the question.

The female Garda that placed her in the room offered her tea or coffee, which she gladly accepted, hoping that it would be accompanied by something to eat, as she was ravenous after the long drive.

The desk sergeant had advised Fiona Moore of the girl's arrival, and Moore left her alone for a few minutes to settle in, before going downstairs to start the interview process.

Chapter Thirteen

"Good morning, Emma," Moore said, taking a seat opposite the girl.

"Now, can I ask you if you know why you are here?"

"No, not specifically, but I guess it's something to do with John's death," Emma Rowe said, trying to keep her voice as neutral as possible.

"Yes, and of course the attack on you at your apartment too. We are trying to establish a motive for these events. So far, we can't see any, except that we know the two incidents are connected. So, we need to try and get to the bottom of whatever's going on. Can you help us with that, Emma?"

"I don't know. I'll try, but I don't understand it either. We were just a young couple working together and planning to get married at some stage," Emma said, her eyes filling with tears at the memory of happier times with John.

Moore paused for a few moments before continuing to allow the girl time to compose herself.

"What can you tell us about John's property dealings, Emma?"

"There's not much to tell. You've obviously found out that he had an apartment that we owned together. That's it, really."

"And where did you get the money to buy that apartment? Is there a mortgage on it?"

"No, there's no mortgage. John paid cash for it. He said he had inherited money from an aunt – his mother's sister, I believe – and that's what he used to pay for it."

"Did you contribute at all?"

"No. I don't have that kind of money, and John was happy to buy it anyway. He was very generous like that."

"And what about the other two apartments? You know, the ones he had put in his father's name?"

"What do you mean?" Emma said.

"Well, I'm sure you know, John owned two other apartments that he had rented out. But he held them in his father's name. Where did he get the money for those?"

Emma looked down at the table, avoiding eye contact with Moore.

"I didn't know. Are you sure they were John's?"

Moore could tell that the girl was holding back.

"Emma, you need to be straight with us about all this. Your life may be in danger, and if we don't get to the bottom of whatever all this is about, we won't be able to guarantee your safety. You can't hide away in Waterford for ever."

This wasn't going the way Emma had planned at all. The police obviously knew more than she thought they would. Maybe she had better change tack.

"I think I might need a solicitor, Sergeant," she said.

"Well, if you think that's absolutely necessary, Emma, but we haven't charged you with anything, and I don't intend to. You're just helping us with our enquiries. But if you insist, I can arrange it," Moore said. She was a bit taken aback by this development. Obviously, the girl had a lot more to tell.

Emma said nothing, so Moore continued with the questioning.

"So, where did John get the money to buy three apartments in Dublin City Centre, Emma?"

"I don't know. He didn't tell me. He just seemed to have an awful lot of cash, and I didn't ask too many questions. I thought he was buying them for his dad. He put them in his father's name, you know."

"Yes, we know. How did he find the apartments? We can't see any dealings with estate agents amongst his papers."

Again, Emma paused as if to think of a suitable answer.

"I found them for him. They were properties where the owner had got into arrears with their mortgage. John bought them cheaply by clearing the outstanding balance, and the owners were glad to get out of it because that way they avoided any court action or increased fees and charges."

"I see. And how did the money for these purchases come into the bank, Emma?"

"Just an electronic transfer – the usual."

"Do you remember from what bank?"

"No, of course not. We get hundreds of these every day, and I never see the details. It was just nice to be able to close some arrears cases cleanly for a change."

"And how did John's father's name come to be on the deeds?"

Emma paused again, but after a few moments, she responded somewhat sheepishly.

"John just signed in Pat's name. He said it was better for tax or something. I don't know. I was just keen to get the cases closed. You've no idea how tricky some of these arrears files can be. Some of them go on for years."

"And did John pay the full amount that the bank was looking for?"

"Sort of. I managed to get him a bit off. The bank often forgives some of the interest and late charges in these situations, so I got him the best price. But the bank was happy with the result."

"What kind of discount are we talking Emma? A thousand? Two?"

"A bit more than that, actually. More like fifteen thousand or thereabouts."

"Wow. So how much did he actually pay for them then?"

"I don't remember the exact figures, but I think the last one was something like one hundred eighty thousand euro."

Moore took out her mobile phone, and using the browser, looked up a website that offered properties for sale in Dublin. She zoned in on apartments in the area where they had visited the Polish girl.

"Those apartments are selling for over three hundred thousand euro, Emma," Moore said turning the phone around so that Emma could see the screen.

"Yes, but he loved me," Emma said and welled up again.

"OK, Emma. I need you to make a statement containing all the information you have given me here this morning. Are you sure you don't know any more about where John got all this money?"

"No, I told you. But if you ask the bank, they'll be able to say where the transfer came from. They keep all that sort of stuff on file for ages. What happens now?"

"You write your statement out, Emma, and then you can go. But we may need to talk to you again. How long are you going to stay in Waterford?"

"I dunno. Another week anyway. Until it's safe to come back to Dublin. You will let me know when you catch whoever it was that broke into my apartment, won't you?"

Moore was impressed with the girl's faith that they would in fact solve the mystery in short order. Moore herself wasn't at all sure that they would. So far, they had precious little to go on. And Moore was no further on in establishing a motive for McKenna's death.

"OK, well you're free to go now, Emma. We may need to talk to you again. I'm sorry that we aren't able to drive you back to Waterford, but the train station is only across the road," Moore said.

"I'll be fine. I'll head over there now. I'm sure there'll be a train along shortly."

* * *

Burke had returned to his desk when Moore arrived back into the main office. She told her boss about the interview with Emma Rowe.

"What did you do with her?" Burke said.

"I let her go. She's gone back on the train to Waterford," Moore said.

"So, are we any further on?" Burke said.

"No, not really. What did you find out from Giltrap?"

"Not a lot. McKenna was managing funds for a number of mostly overseas clients. He was buying and selling unit trusts for them, and there does appear to be something iffy about some of the transactions. Giltrap is looking into it a bit further. That's it, I'm afraid."

Moore told Burke about the conversation she had had with her cousin in London.

"Give him another call. Ask him what sort of wheeze McKenna might have been up to with unit trusts," Burke said.

"Right. I'll call him now."

* * *

"Hi, Mark, it's me again. Got a second?"

"Yeah, sure, Fee. What's up?"

"Well, you know that thing I was talking to you about the other day. Well, we've found out that the person of interest was dealing in unit trusts. Does that help at all?"

"Hmm... could do. I'm not an expert in mutual funds, but I could ask one of my mates here if he knows of anything. I won't mention why I'm asking, and of course no names."

"Would you mind? It could be important. Thanks a lot."

"No worries, Fee. I'll call you later."

Chapter Fourteen

Burke had managed to restrict his alcohol intake to a single pint of Guinness and a small Irish whiskey on his way home from work that evening. It was a lot less than his usual quota, but he was determined to try and get things more under control.

When he opened the door of his house, he was greeted by the smell of fresh furniture polish and disinfectant. He saw immediately that the place had indeed been given a thorough going over by the cleaning company. Gone was the junk mail from the hallstand. Gone was the overflowing kitchen bin that had been crammed with empty pizza boxes and drink cans. The dishes were all washed up and stowed away in the cupboard; all the old newspapers had disappeared; and the downstairs carpets had all been vacuumed thoroughly.

He made his way upstairs, and found that a similar operation had been carried out on his bedroom. His bed was made up with fresh bed linen; all his clothes, which had been strewn around the place untidily, were neatly placed in the wardrobe, and his shirts, now newly laundered and pressed, were folded and placed in an orderly stack on his shelves.

He hardly recognised the bathroom. All the vitreous-ware was gleaming. The shower door, which was supposed to be clear Perspex, but had been stained with soap streaks, now sparkled like the front window of an up-market department store. His various potions and lotions were neatly arranged, and fresh towels were folded and placed over the towel rail above the heating radiator.

Burke was seriously impressed.

Almost afraid to disturb the new-found neatness of the kitchen, he withdrew a frozen lasagne from the freezer, and put it in the microwave to heat up, noting that it too had not escaped the cleaners' thorough treatment. The inside of the machine was like new.

A little while later, when he had eaten and carefully tidied away his dinner plate and cutlery, he cast a critical eye about him. The place was clean, for sure. Probably cleaner than it had been since long before he had purchased it. But it was still dowdy. The floral wallpaper in the sitting room was tired and stained here and there. The swirly pattern on the carpet and the old tiled fireplace belonged in the 1960s. And the curtains which hung limply at the side of the curved front window had simply given up their function.

"Moore was right. This place needs a makeover," he said to himself.

He was still pondering the state of his house when the phone rang.

"Hi, it's me," Fiona Moore said. "Look, I've been talking to my cousin again in the UK. He has a theory about what McKenna may have been up to."

"Interesting, but listen, better not to discuss this on the phone. Any chance you could stop by on your way home. There's something else I want to talk to you about anyway?"

Moore's curiosity was piqued. It wasn't like her boss to invite her to his house. He was a 'strictly business' kind of man, so she wondered exactly what was on his mind.

"Yeah, sure. I'll be there in about twenty minutes, depending on the traffic. Does that suit?"

"Perfect – see you soon."

Moore stopped in a Spar convenience store on the way up to Crumlin. She didn't like to go to her boss's house empty handed, but once inside, she couldn't find anything suitable to buy. There was lots of booze, but that was hardly appropriate given the situation, so eventually she settled on a decent sized box of Butler's chocolates.

She found the house easily and parked outside.

"God, he was right about the house. It does look like a shit-hole," she said to herself as she walked past the rusting wrought iron gates and approached the brown door with its peeling paint. She had little confidence in the old, recently polished bell, so she rapped on the glass panel and stood back.

Burke answered the door a moment later.

"Hi. That was quick! Come in," he said, standing back to let her into the dingy hallway.

"Fancy a tea or a coffee?" he said as they walked through the dark hallway to the kitchen.

"Great, thanks, tea would be lovely."

Moore took in the kitchen in every detail. The presses were straight out of the 1960s, and the gas cooker was from the same era. The floor was covered in what could be linoleum, or perhaps vinyl tiles, and the walls were painted cream, with gloss paint behind the sink and the cooker to make cleaning a bit easier. The furniture was a mixed bag of ancient and modern, with the table covered in green Formica and the four odd chairs painted in much the same colour. The whole thing was, frankly, hideous.

"So, what did your cousin have to say?" Burke asked when the tea had been put down in front of Moore.

"Quite a bit, and I'm not sure if I followed it completely, to be honest. But it seems that units in a unit trust are priced daily. It's called the NAV, or net asset value. Because there are hundreds of thousands of units in a unit fund, each unit has a value that runs to lots of decimal places. The exact number is determined by the system that's being used, but it could be up to fifteen. But here's the thing. The unit value is only displayed to either two or four places. So, there's value in the trailing decimal places that no one sees. The price the client gets is rounded up or down depending on the unseen decimal places. If there's rounding down, then you can skim off the tiny portion to the right of the price that is shown. It's worth very little on a per unit basis, but if you're dealing in millions of units, it mounts up very quickly. The practice is called 'downing' and apparently, it's not all that unusual. Mark said he had read about it when he was studying, and he said some insurance companies make a lot of money from it."

"Wow! So, that could be where McKenna got his wealth. But it raises a lot of questions. Like, for instance, how did he get the money away? How was it not discovered during an audit? And why was he buying and selling so much for some of his clients?"

"Ah, well Mark said the buying and selling would have helped to disguise what he was up to. He'd buy a tranche from a particular fund, strip off the value that we've talked about, and then sell them again on a bid-to-bid basis, whatever that means, so the client wouldn't appear to lose out and the transaction would be very hard to trace. The client might even make some money as well – all the better."

"God, you'd never know what's going on in those bloody banks, would you. Clever though. I wonder if any of this had anything to do with what happened to him," Burke said.

"I know what you mean. I wonder if they knew, or at least had a suspicion?"

"I don't know. Edmund Giltrap isn't exactly forthcoming. But I'll tell you one thing. We need to get back in there first thing tomorrow morning and start shaking the bloody tree. And I don't care who complains about it," Burke said.

"OK. Should we get a few guys from the Fraud Squad to come with us?"

"Not yet. I can probably put the fear of God into them on my own, don't you think?"

"I don't doubt it, Aidan. Oh, and Dónal spoke to the guys that McKenna was out with the night he was killed. They finished up in Spirits Night Club at about one o'clock, and McKenna went off to get a taxi home. They couldn't say what route he was taking."

"Typical. No joy there, then."

"Fraid not. Now, what was the other thing you wanted to talk to me about?"

"Oh, right. Well, believe it or not, I've had this place cleaned up by a firm of professional cleaners. But the thing is, it really needs more. Like redecoration; new carpets and curtains; maybe some new furniture, that kind of thing. And I'm completely bloody useless at all that stuff. I don't suppose you'd be willing to give me a hand, would you?"

"And why do you think I'd be any better at it than you?" Moore said. She was trying to get to grips with a side of her boss that she had never thought existed.

"You're a woman, aren't you?" Burke said with absolutely no sense of irony.

"Jesus, boss. I suppose you'll want me doing the wash up and the ironing next! I think maybe you should get the professionals in," and she stood up from the table to leave.

"I'm sorry, Fiona. No, I didn't mean it like that. It's just men are generally fucking useless at this kind of thing. And I can't afford professionals as you call them. I just need someone to put some ideas forward. I'll do all the work, or get someone in."

"Well, I'm not getting up any bloody ladders, that's for sure. I could suggest a few colour schemes and maybe help you get some new carpets, if you like. Dare I ask what things are like upstairs?" Moore said.

"Worse."

"OK. Let's leave that for now. What kind of a budget do you have to do the place up?"

"Budget? Now you're starting to talk like a bloody banker! I dunno. I guess I could scrape together a couple of grand, but probably not all at the same time. I'm still paying the mortgage on the missus's house, and I had to buy all those new clothes. Is this stuff dear?"

"Curtains and carpets are. And a new kitchen will cost you at least four or five grand, but you can get it on the drip if you like."

"What about paint. Is that cheaper?"

"Yes, I guess. But you need more than paint. Let's see what the sitting room is like. You might be able to paint over the wallpaper there – save you having to strip it all off. That takes ages."

The two went through into the sitting room to assess the décor.

"Did you ever think of opening a window in here? It's very musty."

Burke went to the semi-circular bay window, pulled back the tired net curtain and struggled with the old iron window for a moment to get it open. The hinges were stiff with rust, and he could only manage to open it a few inches.

"See – smells fresher already. Listen, Aidan, if you want me to help, I'll give you a bit of a hand, but it's strictly on a friendly basis – no strings or messing, OK? And don't mention it inside."

"'course. Thanks. You're a star. When do you want to get started?"

"How about Saturday morning. I could drop round about eleven, and I'll bring some colour charts with me. Now, I'd better go."

"OK, thanks again. See you in the morning then," Burke said ushering his colleague to the front door and letting her out.

On the way back to her own nicely decorated apartment, Fiona Moore wondered if she was doing the right thing. It was all very well helping her boss to pick a few pots of paint, but did he have an ulterior motive? She certainly didn't want to get in any way involved with him – these things just didn't work out, even though she had to admit that she did find him quite attractive, in a rugged sort of way.

Chapter Fifteen

O'Dowd was woken by the engine of the van starting up. They had arrived in Holyhead. He recognised the noises of the huge ramp at the front of the ferry being lowered, and drivers returning to their vehicles. If things went to form, the van man would in all probability stop at the large petrol station on the outskirts of the town to fill up with diesel and get some food and drink for the long journey ahead.

He wasn't wrong.

When the driver went inside the shop to get his snacks and pay for the fuel, O'Dowd slipped out the back door. He would spend the night sleeping rough and then get the first train out in the morning to take him to Manchester where he had been before, and had a small number of acquaintances.

He took out his phone and looked at the screen. Nothing.

"I'm not finished with you yet, ye bastard," he said to the instrument.

O'Dowd had had a brief meeting with the man who had ordered the hit on McKenna and his girlfriend. The man wasn't really a 'Mr Big', but he was a bit brighter than

O'Dowd and his contemporaries, and he had a name for being able to put things together. The deal had been mostly arranged with various clandestine phone calls uttered in a sort of makeshift code, but O'Dowd had been assured that the man was good for the five hundred euro he had been promised. You had to keep these things as secret as possible. There may be honour amongst thieves, but not between this lot of ne'er-do-wells.

But O'Dowd was out of pocket, and he wasn't about to let that go. Furthermore, he was now on the run, and while he had been careful not to leave any evidence at the scene of the McKenna killing, he couldn't say the same about the abortive attempt on the girl.

He'd have to lie low in England for a few weeks till it all died down, and then make his way back to sort out the bugger who had shafted him. In a funny way, he was looking forward to that.

O'Dowd didn't know Holyhead well, but he was resourceful, and after half an hour walking around the now deserted streets, he found himself at the entrance to a park. Just inside the locked gates, there was a café and shop. It was a low wooden construction with a broad decking area out front where presumably tables and chairs would be set out during the day for the pleasure of those who liked to take their refreshment outdoors, or perhaps smoke a cigarette.

He had no difficulty getting over the gate, and once inside found a sheltered corner to settle down in. He was largely out of sight, and in any case there seemed to be no one at all around at that time of night. It wasn't cold, so it didn't take him long to doze off.

He was woken by the sound of the chain on the entrance being removed. It was after eight o'clock in the morning, and when he looked out from his hiding place, he saw that it was a bright, clear morning. O'Dowd slipped around the back of the shop while it was being opened and prepared for the day's trade. After a sensible interval, when he saw that the tables and chairs were put out on the decking in front, he went inside and ordered a breakfast of scrambled eggs, toast and coffee. While this was being prepared, he went to the bathroom and tidied up a bit.

After breakfast, he strolled down to the railway station located beside the ferry terminal, and studied the timetable mounted on the wall in a glass case. The journey to Manchester would take almost three hours, and he would need to change trains at Chester.

"Great," he said to himself, "I'll be there by lunchtime."

The train was due in a few minutes, and when it came into the station, O'Dowd waited till the few passengers alighting had gone, and he boarded the last carriage. He had to be careful. Naturally, he hadn't bought a ticket – it was almost sixty pounds after all – so he positioned himself where he could see the ticket collector approaching, and get into the toilet while the inspector passed through. He had done this many times before, and it had always worked for him. The train had fewer passengers than O'Dowd would have liked, but he reckoned he could handle it all the same. And if the worst came to the worst, he would give a false name and address and to hell with it.

But things went better than he expected. Just as the train was about to depart, a rather large woman struggling with two suitcases and a backpack squeezed her way into the carriage that O'Dowd was in. She was puffing and wheezing from exertion, and was having a difficult time managing her extensive cargo. O'Dowd – not normally one to help someone in this situation – seeing that the woman had her train ticket and purse in her hand, got up as if to help. He manhandled the woman's suitcases into the luggage rack at the end of the carriage, for which she was very grateful. The woman more or less collapsed into a seat by the window, and when O'Dowd saw that she was settled and starting to spread her possessions out around her, he got up and walked down the train to the other end. When he too had taken up his new position, he opened his hand to reveal the woman's train ticket.

"That'll do me nicely," he said, grinning to himself, "I could get all the way to London on this one!"

Chapter Sixteen

"Right. Let's go and see the reluctant Mr Giltrap again – just you and me, OK?" Burke said when he arrived in the following morning all full of energy. He was halfway down to his car before Moore caught up with him, pulling on her jacket as she walked.

They drove around to the bank's headquarters building, and as Burke was parking on the double yellow lines outside, his mobile phone rang.

"Get that for me, would you?" Burke said.

"Inspector Burke's phone," Moore said.

"Hi, Sergeant, this is Dónal here at the station. We've had a call from a Mrs Rowe from Waterford. She's very anxious to talk to either you or Inspector Burke as soon as possible. Can you take down her number?"

"Yes, go ahead, Dónal."

The officer called out a Waterford number, and Fiona Moore scribbled it down in her notebook.

When she had finished the call, Burke asked, "What's up?"

"It's Emma Rowe's mother. She wants one of us to call her. Shall I give her a quick ring?"

"Bloody hell, can't it wait?"

"I dunno, it sounded kinda urgent. It won't take a jiffy. I have the number here," Moore said.

"Ok then, get on with it."

Moore called the number that Dónal had given her. The phone was answered immediately.

"Hello, Mrs Rowe. It's Sergeant Moore here from Dublin. You were looking for us?"

"Oh, yes, thanks for calling, Sergeant. I was just wondering when you are going to let Emma go. Her father isn't very well, and he's worried about her," the woman said.

"We have let her go, Mrs Rowe. She was going to catch the train back down to Waterford."

"What time was that, Sergeant?" Mrs Rowe said.

"Mid-afternoon – sometime close to 4:00 p.m. I think," Moore said.

"Well, she never arrived here. Are you sure she said she was coming home?"

"Yes, certain. But she may have changed her mind. Gone back to her apartment or something."

"No, she didn't do that. I called Irene, and she said she hadn't seen her. I hope she's all right, Sergeant."

"I'm sure she's fine, Mrs Rowe. Try not to worry. I'll see what we can find out from this end, and I'll call you back a bit later. In the meantime, ring around her friends and see if maybe she went to stay with someone. She probably didn't want to go back to the apartment after what happened there."

"Very well, but her father's not happy – not happy at all. Will you let us know if you find out anything?"

"Yes, yes, of course. And if she turns up, perhaps you'd ask her to let us know too," Moore said.

"Yes, I will. Goodbye."

"What's the crack?" Burke said when Fiona Moore had finished the call.

"The crack, Inspector, is that Emma Rowe may be missing. She didn't turn up at home last night. Her folks thought we still had her."

"Jesus – that's all we bloody need. What do they want us to do about it?"

"Find the girl, presumably."

"OK. Well, look, I'll go in here and scare the crap out of this lot. Can you get back to the station and start looking for the girl. Keep it under the radar for today, but be thorough," Burke said.

"You mean no press, radio or TV?"

"Exactly. Let's see if we can locate her ourselves first, and remember she's not actually a misper for forty-eight hours, so keep it low key back at the ranch."

"OK, see you later," Moore said as she got out of the car.

She could get a taxi, but it was only a fifteen-minute walk back to Store Street, and although it was cool, it was a bright morning so she would enjoy the walk, and she could use the time to try and process this latest information. Looking at it logically, Emma had been rightly spooked by the attack in her home. It wasn't that easy to get up and down to Waterford, and it was expensive too, so she probably has gone to stay with some friends or relations near Dublin. Moore wondered if they might be able to ping her mobile phone to give them a clue, and then call her flatmates and see if they could point them in the right direction once they had an approximate location. That's what she'd do. When she got back to Store Street, she'd get onto Jane Langford, the tech girl who had cracked McKenna's computer so easily, and ask for her help to locate the phone.

* * *

Burke sat down with Edmund Giltrap in another of the little glass offices at the bank.

"Really, Inspector, this is all getting to be a bit much. I have a very busy day ahead of me, and to be quite honest, we've done all that we can to assist you. I'm sorry about John, but life goes on, you know," Giltrap said.

"For some, Mr Giltrap, for some. Have you finished your rant now?" Burke said.

Giltrap grunted and gave Burke a dirty look.

"Good. Firstly, what have you discovered about where McKenna's money is being held?"

Giltrap shuffled in his seat, and avoiding eye contact with the inspector, said, "We haven't. It's much harder than you think, you know. Can you imagine the number of transactions we process here every day. Talk about a needle in a haystack!"

"Not good enough, Mr Giltrap. Now, to be frank with you, I'm getting mightily pissed off with all this obfuscation and obstruction that you lot are putting up. I'm just this much short of bringing you in and questioning you formally under caution," Burke said, holding up his right forefinger and thumb barely a centimetre apart.

"That's ridiculous. I've done nothing wrong," the man protested.

"Maybe, and maybe not. But your customers might not see it that way if you were escorted from the building in handcuffs by uniformed Gardaí. I'd say it would be certain to make the Evening Herald anyway, and maybe even the RTE news."

"Are you threatening me, Inspector?"

"No, Mr Giltrap, I'm trying very hard to get your co-operation, and so far it doesn't appear to be working too well. So I'm just looking at alternative tactics."

The two men remained silent for a few moments before Burke decided to push on.

"Now, tell me about this 'downing' thing, Mr Giltrap."

"Downing – what downing?"

"You know, where the bank strips off the last eleven decimal places in the value of units, and pockets it."

Giltrap stayed quiet, but Burke thought he could sense the man's complexion reddening somewhat.

"I don't know what you mean."

"Right, OK, have it your way. I'll just pop outside and call the station. Get a car full of uniformed officers up here to take you in," Burke said standing up and taking his mobile phone out of his coat pocket. He turned to leave the little room.

"Wait," Giltrap said, almost pleading.

Burke sat down again.

"Well?" Burke said.

"I have heard of the practice that you mention. But I can assure you, that kind of thing doesn't go on at this bank. It would be more than our lives are worth to indulge in such a practice."

"Maybe that's why John McKenna ended up dead."

Giltrap said nothing.

"Anyway, how would you know? It's almost impossible to detect, as far as my information tells me. And if McKenna was at it, it would explain a lot. Like how he came to own three apartments here in the city that he paid cash for," Burke said.

"I didn't know that. Are you sure?"

"Certain. And I'm surprised you didn't know anything about it. After all, you are, or were, his banker. But more importantly, how can we establish if that's what he was doing?"

"I suppose we'll have to get Internal Audit onto it," Giltrap said.

"I hope that won't take long, Mr Giltrap. We need to get at this information quickly. Maybe we should get some of our forensic accountants in to have a look – see what they can find," Burke said.

"No, no, there's no need for that. I'll get onto it straight away – not that I believe we'll find anything mind you, but we'll certainly look," Giltrap said.

"And while you're looking, I want the names of the clients that McKenna was handling – especially the ones with unit trust investments, and I don't want to have to ask for this information a third time. OK?"

"Yes, OK. I'll get that for you now if you like."

"I like," Burke said. Giltrap got up and left the room.

When he had gone out of earshot, Burke said to himself, "Maybe we're getting somewhere at last."

Chapter Seventeen

Garda Michael O'Carroll left Store Street Garda station after another busy night. He didn't like night duty, but it was part of the job, and it only came around once every six weeks, so he put up with it without complaining too much.

O'Carroll lived in Dunshaughlin, on the border of County Meath. It was the nearest place to the city that he and his partner, Aisling, could afford. She worked for one of the big accountancy firms based along the South Quays, so when Michael was on nights, they didn't see much of each other for that particular week.

To make up for this, instead of going to Connolly Station to get the Dunshaughlin bus home, O'Carroll arranged to meet Aisling at a café on the other side of the river from the Garda station for breakfast. It was still only just after eight o'clock in the morning, so they would have almost an hour together to catch up on each other's busy lives before Aisling was due in work, and in any case, a night of dealing with the policing issues that a busy shift on Dublin's streets threw up certainly gave a man an appetite.

O'Carroll was crossing the river by the new Millennium Bridge. The Liffey was tidal at this point, and when the tide went out fully, mudbanks along the edge of the quay wall were revealed. He glanced down at the dark grey-green water as he crossed the bridge and noticed a lump of what looked like discarded rubbish lying on the mud. But as he focused on the dirty pile, he thought he saw what could be a muddy human hand protruding slightly from underneath it.

The River Liffey was often the site of suicides in Dublin. Indeed, the river accounted for more than ten percent of all the drownings in Ireland every year, and many of these were deemed to be self-inflicted. The casualties were mostly young men, who, for whatever reason, felt that life's travails had overwhelmed them. They jumped in from one of the many bridges along the length of the river from the Phoenix Park to the Custom House during the night, and perished quickly in the black, rancid water. It was members of the Dublin Fire Brigade who then had the unenviable task of recovering the bodies, often at the rate of one or more each month.

Michael called the Fire Station at Tara Street and explained what he had seen.

"I'm not sure if it's a body or not. It could be an animal. But I thought I should let you know all the same," he said.

"Right, we'll come around now. Can you stay put till we get there and show us exactly where it is?" the fire chief said.

"Yes, sure. See you in a few minutes."

Then O'Carroll called his girlfriend and explained that he had been delayed, and why.

"Oh God, that's awful, Michael. Do you think it's a body?"

"I can't tell for sure, but it could be. I'll call you when I know more, but go ahead with your breakfast anyway. I'm going to be tied up with this for a while."

"Don't worry, love. Mind yourself. I'll see you later," Aisling said. She was used to her partner's frequent change of plans at short notice.

Almost as soon as he had hung up from speaking to Aisling, he heard the fire tender's sirens as it sliced its way through the busy morning traffic. The bright red fire engine crossed Butt Bridge and turned right onto Custom House Quay before crossing back over the river and stopping adjacent to the bridge where Michael O'Carroll stood waiting and waving. They pulled the truck to a halt, and Senior Fireman Tim Cawley, whom O'Carroll knew from several other such misadventures, approached.

"Morning, Michael. What have you got for us today?"

"Hi, Tim. It's down there," he said, pointing to the location below on the mud where he had seen the eerie pile.

"Ah, I see it now. I'll get one of the lads to go down and have a look. It might be just a discarded bin bag."

Cawley went off and gave instructions to one of his crew, and O'Carroll watched as the man climbed over the low wall and descended the steel ladder built into the quayside towards the mud. When he got to the bottom, he called one of the other men to let down a hose, and when that had been done, he gently washed the mud away, revealing what was clearly the body of a young woman.

It took two more firemen almost half an hour to get the body clear of the stinking quagmire and back to the dignity of dry land. While this was going on, O'Carroll had called it in to the Garda station, and a squad car with two uniformed Gardaí had arrived at the scene as well as an ambulance. A few curious pedestrians had gathered too, making a small ghoulish crowd that had to be kept back by the police.

As the ambulance men prepared to put the body into a large plastic zip bag to take it to the City Morgue on Amiens Street, O'Carroll asked, "Just a sec, guys. Can I have a look to see if there is any ID on her. It'll save us hours of investigation if we can find out who she is."

"Right you are," the senior paramedic said.

Michael O'Carroll put on bright blue vinyl gloves. He kept a pair in all of his different trouser pockets at all times after being admonished by a detective for touching some evidence a few months back. He then very gently probed the pockets of the dead girl's coat and found a couple of very soggy tissues and a train ticket with much of the text worn away by its time in the water.

He asked the paramedic for a plastic bag, and placed the items carefully inside it before handing it over to one of the uniformed Gardaí, telling him to bring it back to the station and log it. For now, the hapless girl would just be known as 'Jane Doe'.

* * *

Burke arrived at work soon after nine to find his sergeant already at her desk. Just as he sat down, she came into his office holding a small clear plastic bag in her hand.

"Morning, boss. When I was coming in, Terry McDevitt gave me this. There was a body pulled out of the Liffey at around eight this morning, and these were in her pocket. What do you think?" Moore said.

"I think this is becoming far too frequent an occurrence. Do we have an ID?"

"No, boss. Just this sodden train ticket. Her clothes were destroyed, but they may be able to get something more when they remove them in the morgue and clean them up a bit."

"OK. On the subject of missing women, is there any word of Emma Rowe?"

"No, nothing yet. I was going to get on to Waterford to see if she had turned up at home."

"OK. Well, stay on it, will ye?"

Back at her desk, Fiona Moore had an idea. She left the office with the plastic bag still in her hand, and walked the couple of minutes to Connolly Station. She went up the escalator to the ticket office and, presenting her warrant card, asked to see the station master. He was there in the office, and came to the little window immediately.

Moore explained about the train ticket, and asked if they could by any chance tell her anything about it.

"Well, we could run it through our machine here. The magnetic stripe should have a good bit of detail on it. That wouldn't have been destroyed by the water. Give it here and I'll see what we can find out."

Moore handed over the ticket, and the station master walked over to a computer that had a ticket validating device attached. He was back a minute later.

"There you go. It's an adult single to Waterford purchased here yesterday at about five o'clock," he said almost triumphantly.

"Was it bought here at the ticket window, or from a machine?" Moore said.

"From the machine."

"Do you know if that was with cash or a card, by any chance?"

"Almost certainly a card. Well over ninety percent of the transactions for that type of journey are done with cards these days. It's much handier than cash."

"I don't suppose you could match the ticket to the card that was used, by any chance?"

"Well, possibly, but that would take some time. Each ticket has a serial number, and that should be recorded against the debit transaction. But have you any idea how many of these transactions go through our machines every day?" the station master said.

"It's really important. Look, I'll leave you my details, and if you get a chance, maybe you could see what you can do. We may be looking at foul play here."

"OK, leave it with me. I'll give you a call if I come up with anything, but the best we'll be able to do will be the issuer and the card number. I won't be able to get a name."

"That would be terrific. Thanks."

On her way back to the Garda station, Moore decided to stop by the morgue to see if they had had any luck in identifying the Jane Doe. When she got there, she met the pathologist who was just starting to investigate his recently acquired specimen.

Moore introduced herself to the rather dour Doctor O'Higgins, which was hardly surprising given his grim trade. O'Higgins was a tall, gangly man of around fifty with salt and pepper hair, cut short, which accentuated his lean features. He wore rimless glasses, and his steely blue eyes expressed little emotion as he went about his painstaking work.

"Hello, Sergeant. I'm not doing a full post-mortem until later, but I have some preliminary information for you," O'Higgins said.

Chapter Eighteen

Edmund Giltrap was feeling very uncomfortable. He was sitting in an office with a senior member of the Internal Audit team, who was asking some very probing questions about John McKenna's activities.

"So, you're telling me that this young fella, barely a wet week in the bank, had free-go-the-road with billions of our most valued clients' money. Is that it?" the man said.

"No, not at all. There are several controls in place to ensure that nothing untoward happens, and your own team have audited us just last year and found everything in order. Well, more or less, anyway."

The man thumbed through the thick file that he had in front of him.

"Yes, I see it here. I wouldn't agree, Mr Giltrap. There were several non-compliance issues raised in our report. Why, it even says here in audit point 7.2 (a) 'there is no evidence that sufficient attention has been paid to the principle of four eyes on every transaction'. Isn't that right?"

"Yes, but it doesn't say that there is any actual evidence of anything out of the ordinary either. Typical Internal Audit speak for everything's fine."

"I don't think, Mr Giltrap, that it would be wise for you to continue with that attitude under the circumstances. It's clear that McKenna was up to no good, and I intend to discover just exactly what he was doing, and how he managed to syphon off tens of thousands of euro under your beady eye. Unless, of course, you knew about it all along."

"That's an outrageous suggestion! How dare you. My reputation here in the bank speaks for itself, and I won't have you besmirch it, do you hear?" Giltrap said.

The internal auditor remained silent for a few moments.

"Well – a bank official brutally murdered. Piles of money missing, or unaccounted for. We're not talking about the theft of a few postage stamps or some office stationery here, Mr Giltrap. This is a serious business, and I expect your full co-operation as we start to investigate. Is that clearly understood?"

"Yes, of course. I'm as anxious to get to the bottom of this as you are, believe me."

The interview went on in the same vein for another ten minutes. When it was over, Giltrap went to the tea station at the end of the large open plan and made himself a strong cup of coffee. He had some thinking to do.

He recognised that he was between a rock and a hard place. Internal Audit were no pussycats, and had seen off a few of Giltrap's own colleagues over the years for very minor deviations from their ridiculous rules. Their hypocritical mantra 'We are here to support the business' was nonsense, and everyone knew it. But he knew the Gardaí weren't much better. That Inspector Burke was no fool, and he was getting far too close for Giltrap's liking. He had a choice to make, and it wasn't an easy one.

* * *

Moore knocked on her boss's open door when she got back to the station.

"Come in, Fiona. What's up?"

Moore noticed at once that her boss was togged out in a new suit and a well-pressed shirt and silk tie. He looked very handsome in a rugged kind of way, and definitely much improved on his previous somewhat tatty style.

"I've just been round to Connolly Station. The guy there was able to put the train ticket we found in the Jane Doe's pocket through a computer. The ticket was a one-way to Waterford."

"Jesus Christ on a bike! That's all we fucking need. So you reckon it's Emma Rowe?"

"Looks like it. They're doing the PM a bit later on. I'll go back around and see what they can find on the body to confirm the identity, but my guess is that it's her OK."

"Suicide?" Burke said.

"Possibly, though I'm not sure. Maybe her mysterious attacker caught up with her. She must have gone in the river after dark, so what was she doing between five o'clock and, say, eight when she went over the wall? It could be suicide. Let's wait and see what the PM reveals. How are you getting on?"

"I'm just starting to go through McKenna's client list. Grab a seat and I'll show you."

Moore wheeled a chair round to the same side of the table where Burke had papers spread out. As she sat down, she noticed that her boss had aftershave on, which was a definite change and an improvement to his usual rather stale aroma.

"See here," Burke said, pointing to a sheet of green paper covered in figures, "this is the account of a Gregor Zanuk. This guy is loaded, and I don't mean just a bit. He has close to a hundred million invested, mostly in pooled funds. There's a huge pile of transactions against his account, and he's doing very well from it. It's gone up by over eight percent in the last nine months."

Moore looked at the page, not really understanding what she was seeing.

"Where's Zanuk from?"

"Looks like Bulgaria – Sofia, but that may not be his actual address. There is a bank reference here though that puts him somewhere out there."

"Is this it?" Moore said, pointing to the top of the page where 'Bulgarian International Bank of Commerce' was printed.

"Yes, that's it. I'd like to talk to this Gregor Zanuk. See if he recognises these transactions, and how well he knows the folks at our local bank. But it's a bit tricky."

"How so?" Moore asked.

"Well, how do we approach it. Bulgarian police? Through Giltrap? Directly with the Bulgarian Bank? I've never done this sort of thing before. What do you think?"

"Look, give me an hour to research this guy. I might be able to find a way to get directly to him without making waves."

"OK. Nice one."

Moore got up and replaced the chair back in front of the desk.

"Like the new threads by the way. Very sharp," she said, smiling.

"Oh, thanks," Burke said, a little embarrassed by the compliment.

Back at her own desk in the large open plan office, Moore set about her PC to discover all she could about Gregor Zanuk. She was good at this sort of thing, and it wasn't long before she had a nice little dossier on the man and his business activities.

She assembled the various printouts of web pages and the text that she had downloaded, and went in search of Burke.

"I've found out quite a bit about Zanuk. He runs an investment vehicle called Hastavia in Sofia, but it seems to have links well beyond Bulgaria too. It pops up in Athens and Budapest, and they did have an office in Prague, but that seems to be closed now," Moore said when she located her boss.

"I don't suppose you got a phone number?"

Moore smiled at Burke. "Of course I did, silly, but you're not going to call him, are you?"

"That's what telephone numbers are for, isn't it?" he said lifting the receiver of the phone on his desk.

Burke dialled the number, and it was answered by a girl with a greeting that he didn't understand.

"Hello. Do you speak English?" he said.

"Moment," came the response, and the line went on hold with some Slavic music playing rather loudly.

"Hello, how can I help you?" a new voice enquired.

"I was hoping to speak to Mr Zanuk, Gregor Zanuk."

"Who is calling?"

"Burke. Aidan Burke, from Ireland."

"Does Mr Zanuk know you?" the girl asked.

"Is he there, please? I'd like to speak to him."

"Moment," the girl said, and again the music returned. Burke put the phone on loudspeaker.

"Are ye dancing?" Moore said.

"Are you asking?" Burke said, smiling broadly. He hadn't heard that invitation for many years, not since he used to attend parochial hops in the old and draughty shed that passed for a dance hall in his hometown near Port Laoise.

The music finally stopped, and a man's voice came on the line.

"Zanuk."

"Hello, Mr Zanuk." Burke went on to identify himself, explaining that he had his sergeant with him on speakerphone.

"Ah, nice to hear someone from Ireland. How is everything there?" Zanuk asked.

"We're in the middle of an investigation here, Mr Zanuk, concerning some activities at the National Bank. I believe you hold some accounts there?"

"Yes, that's right, we hold quite a lot of money at the bank."

"Do you mind if I ask why you are using a bank in Dublin?"

"Of course. It is the returns, Mr Burke. They get us around eight percent – a very good return in these times. Anyway, why have you called me?"

"I was wondering if I could send you some transactions that have appeared on your account recently by email, and ask you to confirm that they are all correct?"

"Yes, I suppose so. But why not just ask the National bank? I'm sure they can help you, and they are a lot closer."

"If you could just give me your email address, Mr Zanuk, I'll send a spreadsheet across directly and perhaps you could either email me back or call me with confirmation?"

"Yes, yes OK. The email is gregor dot zanuk at hastavia dot bg. I'll have a look as soon as you send them. But do you think our funds are at risk, Mr Burke?"

"No, I don't think so. It's just a small part of our current investigation."

"And what exactly are you investigating?" Zanuk was beginning to sound a little nervous.

"I'm afraid I can't disclose that just at the moment, Mr Zanuk. But we would appreciate your assistance."

"Yes, of course. I have been thinking of making a trip to Ireland anyway to see some of my contacts there, and call to the bank. Maybe this would be a good time?"

"That's up to you, Mr Zanuk, but I would ask you to keep this enquiry confidential for now."

"Oh. OK. Send it then, and we can talk later."

Burke hung up the phone.

"Can you send that stuff off to him right away, Fiona?"

"Yes, sure. I'll do it now. I think our Mr Zanuk is a little bit spooked, don't you?"

"Sounds like it. Let's see what develops."

Chapter Nineteen

Sylvester was back in Store Street Garda station for the second time that week. He's been caught trying to flog the proceeds of his recent shoplifting to an undercover Garda in one of the seedier pubs down the docks.

The detective who was interviewing him was losing patience with this repeat offender, and decided that it was time to take the matter firmly in hand.

"Look here, Sylvester," he said to the miscreant who was smelling rather ripe in the small interview room in the basement of the station. "I've had enough of your shite. This time I'm gonna get you put away for a wee spell. Let's say two years in the Joy."

"Jesus. Just for nicking a few bits out of George's Street. Good luck with that."

"Ah yes, Syl, but this time I have a few more serious crimes that I'm going to put you up for. An assault and a GBH. That should do it."

"You can't do that, ye fecker. That's illegal. I know my rights."

"Don't be daft, Syl. You know how it works. Anyway, you'll be out in a few months, and it's not a bad place to spend the winter. Free food. A nice warm cell and a friendly cellmate to keep you company. What more could you want?"

Sylvester had been in prison before and it didn't go well. They never gave you enough methadone, and some of his cellmates had been a bit too friendly for Syl's liking. He didn't want to go back inside.

"Fuck you. What if I could give you a bit of information?" Syl said.

"Depends. I'm not making any promises, mind. What have you got?"

"Ye know that poor bugger that got stabbed in the lane. Well, I might have some information on who did it. But you need to let me go if I tell you."

"Oh. What information?"

"Have we got a deal?"

"You'll have to give me more. But hold on. I'm going to get someone else to sit in. Don't go away," the detective said ironically.

"Any chance of a cuppa tea?"

"Don't push it, Syl."

The detective left the room and asked the desk sergeant to bring a cup of tea to the young rascal in room three. He then went upstairs to find Fiona Moore.

* * *

"So, Sylvester, what information do you have for us?" Moore asked.

The smell of the young man was really getting to her. It was a pungent mixture of stale smoke, body odour, yesterday's booze, dirty socks and urine. She didn't want to spend any longer than necessary in his company.

"Am I getting outta here?"

"Hold you horses. Tell us what you know, and we'll see."

"The story on the street is it was Anto what did him."

"Who's Anto? What's his other name?" Moore asked.

"I don't bleeding know. Everyone just calls him Anto around here."

The young detective, who spent more of his time than he liked mixing with the low life of Dublin's streets, intervened.

"Is that Anthony O'Dowd?"

"Yeah. That's him, I think."

Moore looked to her colleague.

"He's known to us. Do you know where O'Dowd is now, Sylvester?" Moore said.

"He's fucked off, hasn't he? Gone across the water, rumour has it. I haven't seen him on the streets for a few days anyway. Can I go now?"

"Not so fast, Syl. Why do you think it was this Anto fella that stabbed the man?"

"He was bragging about it in the pub, wasn't he? Said he got a monkey to off the bloke and his bird. Mind you, he'd had a few."

"Did anyone else hear him saying this, Syl?"

"Course. Loads. The boozer was nearly full, and he wasn't holding back."

"Which pub was this, Syl?"

"Ye know – the one down behind Sheriff Street with the blue door. I dunno what it's called."

Moore looked at her colleague, who nodded. He was very familiar with this particular watering hole. It was known to play host to some of the dodgiest characters in town.

"Right, Syl. I'm going to let you go. But if this turns out to be more of your bollocks, I'll personally come after you, and we won't be talking two years either. Understood?" Moore said.

"Sound," Syl said, and got up to leave.

When he had gone, Moore spoke to the young detective.

"Will you check that out for me and let me know. Is Syl reliable, do you think?"

"Probably. But let me confirm it. I'll give you a ring later."

"Thanks, and well done. That enquiry was going nowhere."

* * *

"We've got a name," Moore said as she entered Aidan Burke's office.

"Surprise me. Emma Rowe."

"No, not that. A name for the killer of John McKenna. One of his contemporaries got into a spot of bother and exchanged it for his liberty."

"Cool. And the name is?"

"Anthony O'Dowd, known locally as 'Anto'. I'm just going to check to see if we have anything on him in the system."

Just as Moore was leaving the office, Burke's phone rang.

"Hello, Inspector. This is Dr O'Higgins from the City Morgue. I thought you might like to have the preliminaries on the girl that was fished out of the river."

"Oh, yes, Doctor, thanks. What's the story?"

"Not a good one, I'm afraid. The girl didn't drown. She was dead before she hit the water, or almost dead at any rate. Very little river water in her lungs. And there's more. It looks as if her neck was broken."

"Cripes. Any idea how that happened, Doctor?" Burke said.

"I'm afraid not. But it was violent, and swift. Her head may simply have been rotated swiftly to one side beyond where it's supposed to go, but that's just speculation. There's no sign of any impact though, except for some mild soft tissue bruising which she probably got from the quay wall as she fell. And there's something else. She was pregnant. Not very far gone – less than three months, and of course the baby is lost as well."

"Aw shit, Doc, that's rough. So, you're saying that she was killed deliberately?"

"Yes, it certainly looks that way. A great shame. She was a bonny wee girl with lots to look forward to."

"Just one more thing, Doctor. Was there any identification on the body or with her in her things?"

"No, sorry. Nothing."

"OK, thanks."

As Burke was finishing the call, Moore came back in.

"Well, we have quite a bit of stuff on this Anto. He's got a fairly long list of offences against him, mostly assaults and GBH, that sort of thing. He's quite a vicious little tyke. And he seems to have some known associates in the Manchester area. Maybe he's gone there."

"OK. Well, get onto it, will you? You know what to do," Burke said, dismissing his sergeant.

"Is everything OK, boss?"

"No, not really. I've just had the doc on the phone. If that is Emma Rowe in the morgue, she was murdered. And she was expecting to boot."

"Oh shit. Look, we'd better get someone to ID her as soon as possible. I think I'll get her flatmate Irene in and ask her to do it. We don't want to drag her folks up from Waterford if it's not her. I'm going to rope in one of the others to help out too. This is getting out of hand."

"Good idea. Oh, by the way, are we still on for tomorrow?" Burke said.

"Tomorrow?"

Burke just looked at her and waited for the penny to drop.

"Oh, yes, of course – paint colours and wallpaper samples! Yeah, sure. What time?"

"Eleven suit you OK?"

"Yep, fine by me. See you then."

Chapter Twenty

Moore had drafted Detective Garda Dónal Lawlor in to lend a hand. Dónal was a recent transfer from the uniformed division, but had already impressed the unit with some of his keen-eyed detection work, and he didn't seem to mind working long hours.

Moore put Lawlor to work on getting the body in the morgue identified, and when he had done that, he was to get on to the Gardaí in Waterford and ask them to go out to the Rowes' house and explain that a body had been found in the river, and that it was possible that it might be their daughter. Lawlor would get details of the clothing she was wearing and ask the parents if they thought that they belonged to her, and the guards in Waterford might even be able to get a photograph of Emma from the parents to help copper-fasten the identity.

This was the worst part of a serving Garda officer's job. Somehow, they managed to deal with the fights, the drugs, the thievery, the car crashes and any number of other tragedies that came their way on a daily basis, but when it came to telling a parent that one of their children had been killed, and not in a pleasant way, most Gardaí shuddered at the thought.

Moore then got onto the CID in Manchester. She spoke to an Inspector Kline, and explained that they were looking for an Anthony O'Dowd, thought to be in the Manchester area, and she gave the name of some of Anto's associates that were based in the sprawling city.

Kline asked for a photograph and details to be sent across, and said that they would do what they could, but not to hold her breath.

Two hours later, Kline was back on the phone.

"Sergeant Moore, I think we may have spotted your man here in Manchester. We're trialling some new facial recognition stuff at the Arndale Centre – that's one of our big city centre shopping malls – and it picked him up and matched it to the picture you sent over."

"Nice. Was he apprehended?"

"No, I'm afraid not. We didn't have anyone in the area at the time, but now we know he is here for sure, we'll get him for you sooner or later. Don't worry."

"Thanks for letting me know, Inspector. I look forward to hearing from you again."

"What's this guy done, anyway?" Kline said.

"He's wanted for questioning in connection with a murder here in Dublin. We think he may have stabbed someone."

"Oh, right. Pretty serious then. Anyway, I'm sure we'll nab him soon enough. I'll give you a call when we have him."

"Thanks, Inspector, that would be great."

Moore always marvelled at just how helpful the British police were to their Irish counterparts. After all, Irish men and women had bombed their cities, murdered their soldiers and policemen, and generally made their life miserable for several years in the 1980s, yet the various police forces up and down the country always seemed eager to help out the Gardaí at every opportunity.

Moore went back in to speak to Aidan Burke.

"I'd like to hold a briefing with everyone before we go home tonight. The Super might sit in on it too. Have you got anything more from forensics on the McKenna killing?" Burke said.

"No, sorry, boss. Nothing. The area where the body was found was a cesspit. Far too much spilled beer, piss and everything else you can imagine to be any use. There's no CCTV, and the lads from the bar have been questioned again, but they don't know anything more either. Let's hope the cops in Manchester can lift this Anto fella for us. Anything from Mr Zanuk?"

"No, not yet. But I've sent over the stuff. He should be calling me a bit later."

"OK. Dónal should have a positive ID on the girl soon too. Have you thought about what the motive behind these killings might be, boss?"

"I've thought of little else. I just have a feeling it may be connected to this Bulgarian thing somehow, but why kill the girl? She was hardly involved, unless she's been lying to us heavily."

"We'll never know now, will we?"

"Ah, don't be too pessimistic. Something will break in our direction soon. Wait till you see."

"God, I hope so."

Moore went off to set up the briefing that Burke had requested. She informed Superintendent Jerome Heffernan's office that they would be having it at five-thirty in the Detective Unit's open plan, and that Burke would be leading.

She had no sooner left Burke's office, when his phone rang.

"Hello, Inspector. This is Gregor Zanuk here from Sofia. Thank you for sending over that file."

"Hello, Mr Zanuk. Did you recognise the transactions?"

"No, Inspector. I have checked very carefully. These did not come from here, so there is, as you say, something going on. I am planning to travel to Dublin on Monday along with one of my colleagues and perhaps a representative of the Bulgarian National Bank – our regulator, if I can get hold of the right person in time. Would you be willing to meet with me when I get there?"

"Yes, of course, but you should understand, I am unable to discuss any details of an ongoing investigation with you."

"Of course, that is understood. Don't worry. I'm sure we will find plenty to talk about. I'll call you when I arrive if that's OK?"

"OK. Fine. See you next week."

When he had finished the call, Burke asked Fiona Moore to come back into his office.

"Hi, Fiona. That was Zanuk. He's coming over next week. Look, can you get back onto your guy in London and ask him if he knows anything about this Hastavia lot? I'm beginning to smell a furry rodent."

"Yeah, sure. I'll try and catch him before he goes home. I think they all go off to the pub on a Friday afternoon."

"It's well for some," Burke said.

* * *

"Hi, Mark, it's Fee again. How's it going?"

"Hi, Fee. Pretty good thanks, just about to head off for a few beers. What's up?"

"Well, you know this thing we're working on to do with unit trusts and the National Bank, a new name has come up. They're a Bulgarian investment house called Hastavia. Just wondering if you know anything about them?"

"Hang on a sec, I'll look them up here on our system. Let's see. Is that H A S T A V I A?"

"Yes, that's it. And there's a guy called Zanuk that runs it, we think."

"Oh, wow, Fee, you sure know how to pick 'em."

"Why? What have you found?"

"Well, there's an orange flag against their listing here in our system for starters. That means proceed with caution, or to put it another way, don't touch them. Oh, now I see why. Looks like they deal in a lot of iffy stuff dating back to the Communist era. You know – when everyone was supposed to be equally wealthy, or equally poor. Fat chance. And they are still used as a vehicle for some of the new Russian money too. Nothing here on Zanuk though, but I can root around next week for you if that would be any help?"

"Thanks, Mark. Don't go to a lot of trouble, but if anything obvious pops up, let me know. Now off you go and get pissed."

"You too, I'm guessing. Bye."

* * *

Burke was tidying up his desk before going out into the general office to start the briefing when his phone rang.

"Inspector? It's Edmund Giltrap. We need to talk."

"Good afternoon, Mr Giltrap. May I ask what about?"

"No. Not over the phone. Can you meet me somewhere. Not at the bank. Maybe tomorrow?"

"Hmm. OK. I guess so. Do you know McGill's pub in Clonskeagh – you know the one on the bend in the road? We could meet tomorrow at, say, one-thirty?" Burke said.

"Yes, I know it. Yes, one-thirty would be fine. See you there."

* * *

Burke waited until Superintendent Heffernan had joined the small team in the open plan before starting the briefing. He had asked Peter Byrne, one of the forensics officers, to join them too, and Burke started with him.

"Thanks for coming over, Peter. Can I ask what you got from Emma Rowe's flat?"

"We matched the blood from the attack site to a low life who's in the system – one Anthony O'Dowd, known for a few bouts of GBH and assault. He didn't leave a weapon at the scene – he may have been intending to strangle the girl with a belt from her dressing gown or something. But that's just me speculating."

"Anything else?" Moore asked.

"Yes. We found semen stains on the girl's sheets, and we matched them to the other dead man, John McKenna. That's about it really," Byrne said.

"Thanks. Now, I have some information just in too. Dónal tells me Emma Rowe's flatmate, Irene, has identified the girl that was pulled out of the river as Emma Rowe. So, now we have two murders connected to whatever is going on, but we still haven't got a proper motive," Moore said.

"Oh, and while we're about it, that Giltrap fella from the bank where they both worked called me a few minutes ago. He wants to meet me tomorrow. Maybe he'll be able to help us with the motive for all this. Any luck with locating this Anto bloke?" Burke said.

"Yep! He's in Manchester. The Greater Manchester Police caught him on some new face recognition system they're playing with. They say they'll probably pick him up over the next few days," Moore said.

"Great. OK. Anybody got anything else then? Superintendent?" Burke said.

"Thanks, Aidan. From what you say, the motive is the biggest cause of concern here. There's a fair bit of circumstantial that it's something to do with the bank, but nothing definite. Is that the position?" Heffernan said.

"Yes, sir, that's about right."

"Well, if I were you, I'd lean pretty heavily on this Giltrap guy. It looks to me as if this whole thing is about money, and he works in the bank, so he probably knows what's going on."

"What about your friend Mr McGroarty, sir?"

"Ah, what about him? He's no friend of mine. Anyway, let me deal with him. You just do what you have to do. Follow the money," Heffernan said.

"Thanks, sir. Right, everyone. I'll not be joining you for drinks this evening across the road, I have some, eh, other business to attend to. But don't let me put a damper on things. Off you go."

* * *

Burke drove home through the heavy evening traffic towards his home in Crumlin. It was raining heavily, the gloomy weather reflecting his own sombre mood. He would have liked to go drinking with the team, as he nearly always did on a Friday after work. But he really was serious about trying to reduce his alcohol intake, and the sessions in the bar could go on late into the night, with everyone buying round after round – a cycle it was hard to break out of without suffering derision from the rest of the gang.

On the way home, he stopped off at the local Chinese restaurant and bought a takeaway meal. Once home, he ate it in front of the TV. When he had finished the meal, he treated himself to a single bottle of beer. At ten-thirty, The Late Late Show having failed to deliver anything unmissable on the telly, he threw in the towel and went to bed.

Chapter Twenty-One

Fiona Moore knocked on the door of Burke's house. She was ten minutes early, but she reckoned her boss would be up and about by this time anyway. She had an armful of colour charts for several popular brands of paint that she had collected from a decorating store on the way over.

"Hi, Fiona, come on in. I've got the coffee brewing," Burke said, standing aside to let her into the hall.

"Mmm, smells nice. New coffee maker?"

"Ah, you know. Just something I picked up in one of those sales in the place around the corner. Better than instant anyway."

Moore was amused at the understated way he was speaking about his newfound domesticity.

When she reached the kitchen, she spread the paint charts out on the table while Burke poured her a cup of freshly made coffee and put a few chocolate biscuits on a saucer.

"Now you're spoiling me, Aidan. Go away with your chocolate biscuits, will ya!"

"Ah, go on. You could do with a few extra pounds on you anyway."

"Aidan Burke, stop it, will you? You're embarrassing me!"

"Right, well what about these paints then," Burke said.

"I think a nice pale green or maybe a light, warm grey emulsion in the sitting room would look good. Nice and modern, and you could get an ivory-coloured suite and a pale carpet and it would all look terrific. How does that sound?" Moore said.

"Expensive, that's how it sounds."

"It needn't be. If you like, I'd give you a hand doing the painting. If we did it ourselves, it would save a few bob."

"I thought you said you wouldn't get up a ladder."

"I won't. You can do the high bits, and I'll do the lower sections."

"Are you serious? Would you really?"

"Yeah, sure. Why not? It won't take long with two of us. Then you can get the carpet and the furniture after we've painted the place. I'll give you a hand to pick them out if you like."

"Fiona. Why are you doing this?" Burke said.

"How do you mean? I'm just trying to help a friend, that's all. Can't someone lend a hand without you getting all Hercule Poirot on me?"

"I'm sorry. It's just I'm not used to people doing things for me, that's all. It's nice. Thanks."

"Well, here. Take this colour chart into the paint shop and get five litres of vinyl silk in this colour here – look, I've marked it. And get a paint rolling kit, a roll of masking tape and a couple of, say, two-inch brushes too. That should do it."

"OK. What do we need the brushes for?" Burke said.

"We'll need them for the edges up at the ceiling and down by the skirting boards, around the light switches and door frames, where the rollers don't reach."

"God, listen to you."

"Not just a pretty face you know, Inspector."

"So it seems, and you're right, you do have a pretty face."

Moore let the remark slide and busied herself tidying up the paint charts and putting them back in her bag.

"Now, do you want me to look at any of the other rooms, or have you enough to be going on with?" Moore said.

"Any ideas about the curtains for the front room?" Burke said.

"Oh, yes, sorry, I'd forgotten about those. I was in that big store out on the Ballymount Road last week, and I saw some really nice ready-made ones. I'm sure we could find something there that would go. Let's just measure the windows. Have you got a tape measure?"

"Yeah, there's one in the kitchen drawer, I think."

Burke and Moore spent the next twenty minutes measuring the window in the front room. It wasn't completely straightforward, as the window bowed outwards, and several times they came very close to each other as they manhandled the flexible metal tape around the opening. There it was again – that scent of expensive aftershave. Fiona Moore wasn't sure if it was this that was giving her slight butterflies in her stomach, or just the presence of her boss in this very relaxed and non-working environment. Something was affecting her, that much she knew.

When they had finished planning the re-decoration of the downstairs room of Burke's house, Burke looked at his watch.

"I have to go and meet Giltrap from the bank in Clonskeagh. Fancy tagging along? We could get some lunch after, if you like."

"Yeah, sounds good, but why are you meeting him on a Saturday?"

"I'm not sure what's on his mind, but we need to find out. Don't you agree?"

"Definitely. Let me just wash my hands and then let's go. I'll leave the paint cards here for now in case you want to browse some more."

"Great."

* * *

They arrived at McGill's pub at just after one-twenty. McGill's was a popular place that served food all day, and was spread out over two floors with a small beer garden at the back that was formed with decking suspended over a tributary of the Dodder River. The pub attracted a strong rugby crowd, but there was no match on today, so the several large screen TVs that were dotted around showing various different sports were turned well down.

Burke and Moore walked through the place to see who was about, before settling down at a four-seater table in front of the open fireplace near the door to the front of the main lounge. As soon as they were seated, a young girl dressed in black jeans and a black T-shirt with 'Staff' emblazoned in large white writing front and back approached carrying two menus.

"What would you like?" Burke asked his partner.

"Just a sparkling water for me," Moore said.

"That's two, please," Burke said to the girl and she scurried off to fulfil their order. She was back a couple of minutes later with two glasses with ice and a slice of fresh lime, and two bottles of sparkling water straight from the fridge.

The girl started to open the bottles to pour out their drinks, but Burke stopped her, telling her that it was OK, they'd do that themselves.

They had just taken a sip of the cool, refreshing drink when Giltrap came in.

Burke had positioned himself facing the door, and as soon as he saw the man, he stood up and raised his hand.

Giltrap came across and sat down.

"I wasn't expecting both of you," Giltrap said, a little nervously.

"That's not a problem, is it?" Burke said.

"No, no, it's fine."

The ever-attentive lounge girl was back at the table having seen the new arrival.

"What can I get you?" Burke asked.

"A pint of Heineken please."

The girl heard the man and didn't need to be told twice, so she disappeared again.

"Do you live out this way, Mr Giltrap?" Moore said, keen to break the ice.

"Me? Oh, no, not really. I'm in Sandycove, but I was brought up in Milltown, so I know the area pretty well. We used to come here when I was a student for the rugby matches. Those were the days."

Burke wasn't one for small talk, so he cut in.

"So, Mr Giltrap, what brings us all here on a Saturday afternoon that's so important?"

Giltrap took a mouthful of his lager. He put down his glass, and looked nervously at Fiona Moore.

"Well, Inspector, I'm afraid I haven't been completely honest with you. I haven't exactly lied, but I've been a bit economical with the truth."

"Oh? Go on." Burke said.

"Yes. John McKenna and I had a sort of arrangement, you see. I knew he was messing about with some of the client accounts. Mind you, I never knew the details – well, not the minor details, anyway. But I did know that he was making a bit of money from it. He assured me that the clients weren't being disadvantaged, and that his little scheme could not be discovered."

"I see. And what were you getting out of it?" Burke said.

Giltrap shuffled in his seat, and took another drink.

"It's a bit awkward. But I may as well tell you, I suppose. He used to let me use one of his apartments from time to time."

"For what?" Burke asked.

"I used to bring a woman there occasionally. I'm married, you see, and well, you know…"

Moore had to stifle a giggle. Giltrap was in no way attractive, or so she thought, and how he managed to get a bit on the side was beyond her. But, she supposed, there was no accounting for taste. Maybe his occasional partner was equally unattractive.

"No money changed hands between you and McKenna?" Burke said.

"No, nothing like that. I just turned a blind eye to his carry on. I hope my wife doesn't have to find out, does she? She'd kill me."

"Maybe not. But listen, have you any idea how McKenna got his ill-gotten gains out of the bank? We can't find any account belonging to him that is stuffed with money."

"That's not a mystery, Inspector. Very easily, as it happens. He just sent the proceeds out to a chain of banks all around Europe, and back to an account in his father's name. His father knew nothing about it, of course, but John was able to use the funds once they came back in."

"But these were small amounts, just lots of them. Did he not lose a lot in the various bank transfers?"

Giltrap smirked.

"No, he didn't lose anything. We have special codes we can attach to certain transactions telling the receiving bank not to apply a charge. And it was all in euro anyway so there was no currency risk involved. And small transactions don't attract scrutiny from regulators. Even though it was crooked, I have to admit, he was a very smart lad."

"Have you any idea how that might have got him killed?" Moore asked.

"No, none. His clients are all corporate entities. I doubt they would be involved in any violence, even if they had found out, which they probably didn't anyway."

Moore looked at Burke and he nodded imperceptibly.

"I think you should know, Mr Giltrap, that Gregor Zanuk from Hastavia will be here next week. He certainly is aware that someone was fiddling with his investments, so I imagine you'll be seeing him."

Giltrap paled noticeably, and took another swig of his lager which was going down quite quickly.

"But tell me, Mr Giltrap, why have you come forward with this information now?" Burke said.

"Guilty conscience, I guess. I couldn't bear to think that I was in any way instrumental in his demise. And then of course there's Emma Rowe too."

"But how could you be responsible for what happened to McKenna, or Rowe for that matter?" Moore asked.

"Just by letting him get away with it. I should have stamped it out and had him fired as soon as I discovered what was going on. But I was selfish, and now look what's happened. What will become of me?"

"That's not up to us. From what you've told us, you haven't actually committed a crime, unless you have more to tell. Are you sure you didn't benefit financially from what McKenna was up to?" Burke said.

"No, I didn't. Not a penny."

"Well then, it's up to you. You have to decide whether to tell your Internal Audit department all you know, or to act surprised when they uncover it. Hastavia don't seem to have lost out, but I doubt they'll keep their account with the National. We need to find out why these two young people have been murdered, and by whom. Any ideas?"

"No, none at all. But if anything else comes to light, I'll tell you. Promise."

Just as Giltrap was getting up to leave, Moore had an idea.

"Before you go, Mr Giltrap, I wonder of you would allow us to examine Emma Rowe's office computer?"

"It's a bit unorthodox, but I guess it would be OK. You'll need to be discreet. Send someone in on Monday and get them to ask for me. I'll bring it into my office, and they can examine it there."

Giltrap finished his pint and left the two detectives pondering what they had learned.

"Ever the banker. Let's get something to eat. I'm starving," Fiona Moore said, picking up the menus that the waitress had left earlier.

Chapter Twenty-Two

The bank was a busy place on the following Monday morning when Jane Langford arrived to inspect Emma Rowe's PC. She asked for Mr Edmund Giltrap, as instructed, and a few minutes later he arrived to meet her in reception.

When introductions had been made, Giltrap said, "Come on up to my office, Miss Langford. I have to see a client, but I can leave you with the computer. What are you hoping to find?"

"If I knew that, I wouldn't have to look, would I?" she said.

Giltrap didn't respond. He was preoccupied with the meeting with Zanuk that was to come in a few minutes.

Giltrap's office was modern, and relatively tidy if not capacious. Like all the other offices in the bank, it had glass walls – apparently a policy that had been introduced to minimize the opportunity for any kind of molestation between any two persons having a private meeting. Despite the construction, it appeared to be relatively soundproof, so that when the door was closed, the hubbub of the open plan just outside was largely silenced.

Langford assumed that the soundproofing worked both ways.

Emma Rowe's PC had been arranged at the edge of Giltrap's desk and, by the looks of it, had been connected to the bank's LAN. It still had a tiny fluffy animal stuck to the top left hand corner of the display. The PC's display had a screen saver twirling around on it, and a request for a login password in the centre.

"What's the password, Mr Giltrap?" Langford asked.

"I've no idea. That's why they brought you in, isn't it?" he said sourly.

"Did Emma have a diary?"

"I imagine so. I don't really know. If she had, it will be in her desk drawer," Giltrap said.

"Perhaps you could show me which is her desk, please?"

"Very well. But that's all the help I can give you. I have an important meeting in a few minutes. Come along then."

Langford followed Giltrap through the maze of white workstations that were arranged on the floor, to the stairs where they descended one flight and into the mortgage department. Emma's desk was quite close to the door, and Langford found the key in the drawer of the small pedestal unit tucked underneath the work surface. Langford easily located the little black A5 sized diary and held it up to show Giltrap who nodded, indicating his assent for her to take it with her.

Back in Giltrap's office, Langford thumbed through the diary. She could see that Emma Rowe had changed her PC password regularly, presumably to comply with the bank's security procedures, but on each occasion she had written the new password into the book with a couple of characters from the word replaced with dashes. This would act as an *aide memoire* for her should she forget the current one. It wasn't hard to fill in the blanks, as Emma's passwords were the titles of popular songs of the time.

Langford turned to the PC and entered the password with the missing letters included, and the PC sprang into life.

Langford spent the next hour and a half exploring everything she could find on Emma Rowe's computer. Several of the programmes were purely bank-related, and some needed further passwords which she didn't have. Therefore, a good deal of her time was spent scouring the email application. In addition to the bank's own email account, Emma had grafted in a personal Hotmail account into the Outlook client that the bank used. This account contained a number of folders, and it wasn't long before Langford found an email trail that she followed back through several months of interaction.

* * *

Gregor Zanuk had been shown to a much more luxurious office on the seventh floor of the modern bank headquarters and had been plied with coffee, biscuits and spring water before Giltrap arrived accompanied by a rather stern looking woman in her late forties from Internal Audit, and a young man from the legal department who looked very uncomfortable, and quite out of his depth.

When introductions had been made, Giltrap addressed the meeting.

"Mr Zanuk. Of course, it's always a pleasure to welcome our more prestigious clients to the bank. On this occasion, I hope you have not had to travel here in vain. We have studied your various accounts, and can see that while there may have been some slight irregularities in the way they were managed, you haven't lost anything as a result, in fact, quite the opposite. You have probably gained from them."

"Mr Giltrap. I think you are missing the point. My own clients are from a wide and varied background. My business, and my relationship with them relies entirely on trust. They expect, and I do too, that our affairs will be handled with the utmost probity. Any irregularities, as you call them, simply cannot be tolerated. If my clients were to hear of these matters, I would probably have to close my business, and I could suffer much worse consequences too."

The meeting progressed along these lines for well over half an hour, with Zanuk questioning everything from the integrity of the organisation to the method by which they selected their staff, and Giltrap attempting to rebut all of the innuendo and allegations, although he was quite obviously struggling with the delicate situation.

Feeling the need to change direction, the young lawyer decided to intervene.

"And who exactly are your clients, Mr Zanuk?" he said.

"That's none of your business, young man. As far as the bank is concerned, I am your client. That's all you need to know."

"Not quite, I'm afraid," the young man said, gaining a little in confidence. He went on, "You see, the bank has a responsibility to ensure that any monies held here are from completely unquestionable sources. Otherwise, we would be left open to some very serious sanctions from our regulator."

"Just what are you suggesting?" Zanuk said coldly.

Giltrap intervened.

"We're not suggesting anything, Mr Zanuk, but my colleague is correct. We do need to be satisfied that the provenance of these funds is beyond question."

Zanuk remained silent for a moment and then spoke up.

"My clients come from various Eastern European countries. They entrust their funds to me as I can deliver discretion, security and a reasonable return on their cash. Yours is not the only institution where I have funds deposited, Mr Giltrap, and now, because of this incident, I may have to reconsider."

Giltrap wasn't put off by the implied threat, and went on.

"Would any of your clients be based in Russia, Mr Zanuk?"

"Mr Giltrap, I'm not here to be interrogated. I would like to proceed to the matter of compensation. I have other business to attend to in Dublin as well, you know."

Giltrap said nothing, and waited.

Zanuk, uncomfortable with the silence, responded.

"As you mention it, yes, some of my clients are Russian-based, but I don't see what that has to do with anything."

It was time for the rather dour woman from Internal Audit to have her say.

"Mr Zanuk, given all that has gone on, please remember that we have lost two of our employees to violent crime, and while there is no suggestion that this has anything to do with you or your clients, it is a coincidence that at least one of them was working directly, and almost solely, on your accounts. Given what has transpired, it is the bank's view that it might be best if you found another institution to hold your funds. That would save us all a lot of further inconvenience. The Irish police are taking a keen interest in these cases, and it won't be long before they latch on to the money that McKenna was managing and where it came from, if you understand me?"

There was silence in the room while this bombshell was assimilated. The Internal Audit lady, sensing the opportunity, pressed on, "And as to the matter of compensation, that's completely out of the question. As it is, we will have a substantial pay out to Mr McKenna's family under our 'death in service' benefits arrangements."

Zanuk was dumbfounded. So much so, that he didn't actually know how to react. He gathered his papers together, and made ready to leave.

"Mr Giltrap, you have not heard the end of this, I can assure you. I am not without influence in certain quarters, believe me. I will not let this go. You will be hearing from my lawyers."

Chapter Twenty-Three

"Come in, Jane, take a seat. Hang on, I'll just get Sergeant Moore to join us," Burke said, leaving the room to collect Fiona Moore.

When the three of them were back in his office, he said, "Well, Jane, did you find out anything from Emma Rowe's PC?"

"Yes, I did, sir. Quite a lot, as it happens."

"Well, let's have it then. Don't keep us in suspense."

Langford went on to explain about the personal email account that she had uncovered on Rowe's computer.

"I managed to take a copy of the whole folder on this USB stick. But the gist of it is that going back to the year before last, Emma had a different boyfriend, a Derek Cotter. There are lots of email exchanges with him on her Hotmail account. But here's the interesting thing. Towards the end, when things were going badly between them, Cotter became very unpleasant. He was calling her names – not nice names, and there were some thinly veiled threats against her too, like 'you'll be sorry', that sort of thing."

"When did these messages end, Jane?" Moore asked.

"A couple of months ago. Emma had stopped communicating with him some time before that, but he kept on harassing her, and some of the emails are, well, frankly, a bit unsavoury. I'll get them all printed out and you can see for yourselves."

"Do we have this Cotter fella's address?" Burke asked.

"No. But I have an IP address for where the emails were sent from. It shouldn't be too hard to track him down. And there's more."

"OK," Burke said.

"I looked through the internal emails between McKenna and Rowe as well. It looks to me that she knew very well what McKenna was up to. There's one email that is particularly damning. It says something like 'I just have to do a few more turns, and then we'll have enough for number three,' which I assume is the third apartment that they bought together."

"Wow. So it looks like they were in it together?" Moore said.

"Looks like it, yeah."

"OK. Thanks, Jane. That's good work. Can you print out anything that you think is relevant, and I'll read over it all later. And when you're done, leave us the memory stick, won't you? And see if you can match up that IP thing – we need to speak to this guy Cotter."

"OK, sir. I'll get on then," Langford said and left the office.

* * *

"What do you make of all that?" Moore said.

"The more I learn about this case, the less I know. It's a right fucking puzzle. Have you any thoughts?"

"No more than you. But give me some time with those emails, and something may dawn on me. What are you going to do?"

"I think I'll give our new best friend Mr Giltrap a call. I think he said he was meeting the guy from Hastavia today.

He may have picked up something interesting. And I want to thank him for facilitating Langford as well. He didn't have to do that," Burke said.

* * *

"Mr Giltrap, it's Inspector Burke here from Store Street. I just wanted to call and thank you for facilitating our technical officer today. That has been most helpful," Burke said.

"Oh, you're welcome, Inspector. She was no trouble really. Did she get anything useful from Emma's PC?"

"Maybe. We need to do a bit more investigation to be sure. May I ask if you have ever heard the name Derek Cotter?"

"Cotter, no, I don't think so. Who's he?"

"Just a name we came across. It doesn't matter. He doesn't work at the bank then?"

"No, I don't think so. I don't know everyone here of course, and then there are all the branch staff, but I can ask HR if you think it's important?"

"It's OK. I'll get back to you if I need it followed up. Anything else strange?"

"Well, we had a meeting with Mr Zanuk of Hastavia earlier. He did say one thing that could be of interest. He told me that some of his clients were Russian, but I don't know if that's relevant. It's just you hear so many bad things about them these days."

"Yes, I know what you mean. Well, thanks anyway. I'll call you back if I need a follow up on Cotter."

"Righto. Bye."

Burke went in search of Moore whom he found pouring over pages and pages of closely typed emails at her desk.

"Guess what, Fiona," he bent over and whispered in her ear.

"What?"

"Turns out some of the money that McKenna was fiddling with belonged to Russians!"

"Are you thinking what I'm thinking?" Moore said.

"Russian money – Russian blade. Coincidence?"

"Exactly!" she said.

"Is it generally known that the knife that killed McKenna was Russian?" Burke asked.

"No. We didn't release that to the press."

"OK. Well, let's keep it that way. How are you getting on with this lot?"

"It's interesting. Emma and Cotter were definitely an item at one stage. Then it looks as if something happened and she went off him, but he didn't take it well. I'm still going through the emails, but he seems to have got very bitter about it. Some of these are nasty. I'll be finished in about another hour, and I'll draw up a summary."

"OK. Cool. I'll see if I can find anything about Derek Cotter. Jane should have deciphered the internet thing by now."

Burke went in search of Langford and found her at a desk working with two separate PCs.

"Hi, Jane. Did you find out where Cotter's emails were coming from?"

"Yes, sir. They must have been sent from his workplace. It's a small financial brokerage out in Blackrock. It's called Omega First Financial. Here's the details," she said, handing him a slip of paper.

"Thanks, Jane."

Burke went back to his office and called the number Langford had given him.

"May I speak to Derek Cotter, please?" he said to the girl who answered the phone.

"Who's calling please?" she said.

"My name is Aidan Burke."

"Hold on please, Mr Burke."

The phone system started to play music as Burke drummed his fingers impatiently on the desk. A moment later, a man's voice came on the line.

"Mr Burke, how can I help you?" the man said.

"Is that Derek Cotter?"

"No. I'm sorry Mr Cotter no longer works for us I'm afraid. May I ask what it is in connection with?"

Burke introduced himself and asked to whom he was speaking.

"It's Malcolm Smith. I'm the senior partner here. May I ask in what connection you are calling, Inspector Burke?"

"Derek's name has popped up in an enquiry we are pursuing here, Mr Smith. Do you know where he is working now?"

"I'm afraid not. Look, Inspector, Cotter didn't leave of his own free will. We had to let him go, and without a reference as well."

"I see. Why was that?" Burke said.

"Well, without going into detail, there was some inappropriate behaviour which came to my attention, and we won't tolerate any of that sort of thing here. We could be sued silly, you know."

"I see. Well, maybe you could just give me his home address, Mr Smith?"

"Hold on, Inspector, I'll just look it up here in the system. Yes, here we are. He was living at Apartment 128, The Moorings on Grand Canal Dock."

"You said 'was' Mr Smith. Do you know if he's moved on from there?"

"I haven't a clue. But that's where we sent his P45 in any case."

"Was Cotter a good employee?"

"At first, yes, he was excellent. Our clients loved him, and he brought in a good bit of business. But as time went on, his performance deteriorated. Then he got into a few rows with some of the other people here. It got quite unpleasant on a couple of occasions. To be honest, I was glad to see the back of him."

"OK, well thanks for your help. I may be back in touch if we need to find out more."

"That's fine, Inspector. Glad to have been useful."

Burke went back out to where Fiona Moore was just finishing with the stack of emails.

"C'mon get your coat. We're doing house calls again."

* * *

Burke and Moore drove out to Grand Canal Dock and parked up near the Bord Gáis Energy Theatre. They found The Moorings easily. It was a modern block overlooking the harbour, constructed over seven floors. Each apartment had a balcony, and some of the occupants were even sitting out, despite the coolness of the afternoon.

They climbed the stairs to the first floor, and found apartment number one hundred twenty-eight at the very end of the corridor. Moore rang the doorbell, which had a small paper label beneath it with the name Ryan written in black felt-tipped pen.

They could hear music coming from inside the apartment, and after a moment the door was answered by a girl dressed in a brown polo neck sweater and black jeans. Her hair was tied off in a ponytail.

"Yes, can I help you?"

Moore held up her warrant card, and told the girl that they were looking for Derek Cotter.

"He doesn't live here anymore. He must have been a previous tenant, because I still get some mail for him. Mostly circulars and junk," the girl said.

"Did he live here with you?" Burke said.

"Oh, no. I never met him."

"I presume he didn't leave his address in the flat for you to send on his mail?" Moore said.

"No. I don't know where he's gone."

"Who do you rent from?" Moore asked.

"It's a firm of estate agents in town. Millers on Dawson Street."

Moore made a note of the name in her pocket book.

"What's your name?" Burke asked. He seemed to be getting quite fed up with this dead end.

"Ann Cleary."

"OK, thanks, Ann. If by any chance Cotter calls around or contacts you, please give us a call, and try to find out where he's living now. OK?" Moore said, giving the girl her card.

"Yes, OK. But what's this about?" Cleary said.

"Just a routine enquiry. Thanks."

On the way back to the car, Moore asked her boss what he thought.

"Ah, I don't think we need bother about this Cotter fella. It's a bit of a long shot anyway, a few nasty emails from a spurned lover doesn't amount to much. Let's focus on finding McKenna's killer."

Chapter Twenty-Four

O'Dowd was getting on pretty well in Manchester. He had accumulated quite a bit of cash, mostly from shoplifting, and operating his well-practiced ATM scam late at night, when the unfortunate bank customers were often a little worse for wear from drink.

For the shoplifting, he concentrated on high-end electrical stuff, like laptop computers and expensive phones. His mates had introduced him to a couple of fences in one of the city's seedier pubs, and he was able to clock around seventy to a hundred pounds a time for most of the items.

But the fact that there was unfinished business back in Dublin was bothering him. He kept thinking about the five hundred euro he was owed for taking care of McKenna and his girlfriend – although he hadn't actually killed the girl, as he was supposed to. He wanted to get back to Dublin, find out who the mystery man that had ordered the killings actually was, and pay him a visit.

With his newfound prosperity, O'Dowd made a decision that would prove to be fateful. He no longer wanted to stow away in the back of some smelly truck to get back home, so he decided that he would buy a ticket on Ryanair instead. He'd never actually been on an aeroplane, so he was looking forward to the experience. With the help of one of his mates, he used his new, stolen phone to make the booking using the Ryanair app. He chose a flight at six forty-five in the morning on Saturday, calculating that this would be the least crowded for the day, and in any case it was also the cheapest at just nine pounds ninety-nine. O'Dowd didn't have a credit card, but his mate paid for the fare with his, and he reimbursed him with a crisp new tenner that he had acquired whilst standing behind a young girl at an ATM a few nights previously.

He wasn't used to being up at the early hour demanded by his dawn flight, and as he had been warned to be at the airport in good time. He rose at four o'clock in the morning and walked to the train station where services to the airport had just commenced. He even bought a ticket to travel on the train, which was very unusual for him, but he didn't want anything to delay him that morning.

When he got to the airport, he marvelled at the massive array of glitzy shops that adorned the departure lounge. In the centre of the huge open space, there was a stand with a silver Mercedes sports car turning slowly around, and electronic flashing signs announcing that this fabulous car could be yours for just twenty-five pounds.

"Feck that," O'Dowd said to himself, "I could get one of them for nothing back home, bloody chancers."

He bought a cup of strong coffee from the stall nearby, and sat down close to the departures board, waiting for the gate to be displayed for the Ryanair flight to Dublin. The place was actually quite busy, and he marvelled at the number of people that would get up at such an ungodly hour for a flight.

At five past six the screen in front of him blinked and showed that his flight would depart from gate 140. O'Dowd looked around to see if he could see the gate anywhere, and finally located a sign saying "Gates 101-150

– 5 mins" and an arrow pointing down a long brightly lit corridor.

When he arrived at gate 140 a few minutes later, he saw that his fellow passengers were all standing in two separate lines in front of the door to the plane. There was a sign at the front of one line saying 'Priority Boarding' which O'Dowd didn't understand, so he stood at the back of the shortest queue and waited.

After a few minutes, two Ryanair girls in blue uniforms arrived, and the doors to the outside opened. Passengers started filing through. When O'Dowd got to the top of the queue, he presented his boarding pass which the girl scanned using some kind of electronic wand. The machine to which it was connected beeped loudly and persistently, and when the girl looked at the screen to which the thing was connected, she nodded to a security man who was standing nearby. The man came over.

"Mr O'Dowd, could you just stand aside for a moment please and let the other passengers pass."

"What's up man? I got my ticket and all here," O'Dowd said, waving his boarding pass in the man's face.

The security man, who was stockily built and rather grim-faced, put his hand on Anto's elbow and directed him out of the line to the side by the terminal window. Before O'Dowd realised it, he was joined by two other security guards, and O'Dowd was boxed in – just in case he decided to make a run for it.

The security man that had approached O'Dowd first spoke quietly into his radio.

"What the fuck is going on. Let me go! I'll miss me bleedin' flight," he said in vain.

"That's the least of your worries, pal," the man said with a smirk, and they ushered Anto away to a small and very stuffy room with a 'Security' label on the door.

After another half-hour, by which time the Ryanair Boeing 737 was at fifteen thousand feet above the Irish Sea, two uniformed policemen arrived in the little room and took O'Dowd away. He protested loudly of course, accusing his captors of everything from mistaken identity to racism, but it had little effect. They had heard it all many times before.

* * *

It took Manchester Police most of the day to process O'Dowd. He was interviewed at length, at first denying any wrongdoing of any kind, but slowly having to admit to a number of muggings and other crimes as video evidence was produced.

It was nearly five o'clock when the detective sergeant who had been leading the interviews contacted Inspector Kline to appraise him of the position and ask for advice.

"Hi, guv. We have that little Irish toe rag down here. We've got him on a number of charges, and he's even admitted a few of them too. He didn't really have much choice. What do you want me to do with him?"

"Why don't you find a nice uncomfortable cell to put him in overnight. We can get a statement from him in the morning, and then we'll probably bail him. But I'll give the Paddies a call and see if they want to come and collect him. Best to get him outta here if we can, we have enough of our own to deal with."

"Right, guv. Cheers."

Kline got through to Aidan Burke at the first attempt.

"Inspector Burke, it's Freddie Kline here from Manchester CID. How's things?"

"Oh, hello, Inspector. Yes, not so bad thanks. What can I do for you?"

"Well, we have your lad O'Dowd here in custody. We're going to charge him with a few muggings and a bit of shoplifting. But we'll be bailing him tomorrow. If you like, we could bail him into your custody on a Section 94," Kline said.

"Oh, yes please. I can get a couple of Gardaí over to you in the morning to collect him if you like?"

"Why don't we deliver him to the airport for you. We can do a ramp transfer so he doesn't have an opportunity to run for it. What do you think?"

"That would be terrific. Thanks very much, Freddie. I'll set it up, and let you have the details overnight. Can I have your email?"

Kline gave him the email address which Burke duly noted on his jotter.

When the call was over, Burke called Moore into the office and asked her to make the arrangements for the repatriation of Anthony O'Dowd.

* * *

It was almost seven o'clock by the time Fiona Moore had made all the arrangements with the airline and two detectives for Anthony O'Dowd's collection from Manchester. Two of them would travel out on the early morning Aer Lingus flight to Manchester, collect O'Dowd and travel back on the same plane to Dublin. Aer Lingus had, as always, been most helpful, and they had arranged for the three to sit in the front row of the aircraft on the return journey, and as the flight was only about half full, several rows adjacent to those reserved for the Gardaí would be left empty. O'Dowd and his escorts would be boarded last to avoid any embarrassment to the other travellers, and with a bit of luck, no one would notice what was going on at all.

Burke found Moore at her desk tidying up her papers.

"All sorted, boss. He'll be here by half-ten or eleven in the morning," Moore said.

"Great. Thanks, Fiona. I've told the Super and he seems happy enough, even though we haven't any forensics to tie the lad to McKenna's death. But we should be able to sweat it out of him using the stuff from Emma Rowe's attack."

"I'm looking forward to it already. Oh, by the way, did you get the paint?"

"Paint? Oh, no, Jesus, I totally forgot. But I have the list here somewhere," Burke said fumbling in his pockets for the slip of paper where he had written the paint codes down.

"It's OK. Would you prefer to leave it for another time? We don't have to tackle it this weekend."

"No, no, let's do it if you're still up for it?"

"Yeah, sure. You get the stuff, and I'll call around at about eleven on Saturday in my painting gear!"

"Thanks. I'll stop off on the way home tonight and get it then."

"OK, see you tomorrow."

Chapter Twenty-Five

As arranged, Anthony O'Dowd arrived at the Garda station shortly before eleven the following morning. Moore had been busy writing up her notes in the PULSE system and hadn't noticed the time slip by. When she got the call from the front desk advising her that the prisoner had arrived, she went looking for Inspector Aidan Burke.

Burke wasn't in his office, so she asked around to see if anyone had seen him that morning, but drew a blank. She went back to her desk and called Burke's mobile phone. It rang ten times before being answered by a very hoarse, gravelly voice.

"Burke."

"Inspector. Is that you? It's Fiona. Where are you? O'Dowd is here and we're supposed to be questioning him."

"Oh, shit. Look, I'll be there in a few minutes. Wait till I get there," and he hung up.

"Christ, he sounds rough," Moore said to herself as she replaced the receiver.

Twenty minutes later Burke arrived at the station. He was in a crumpled suit and a creased and slightly stained shirt, and he hadn't shaved.

"Hi, Fiona. Sorry about that. Where's yer man?"

"Look, boss. Why don't I start off with Dónal? Give you a chance to, eh, freshen up, maybe get a cup of coffee. What happened anyway?"

"What do you mean? Oh, sorry, right. I went into Nugent's on the way home last night, and we kinda got stuck in."

"Right, well you'd better get sorted for a few minutes. We're in interview room three. Come down when you're feeling a bit better."

Burke didn't argue. He knew he was a mess. He hadn't meant to stay so long with his old cronies last night, but they were buying rounds and he kind of lost track of the time, and had had what is often referred to as a 'right skinful'. He wasn't proud of himself.

Moore took Detective Garda Dónal Lawlor with her to interview room three. O'Dowd had been joined by a duty solicitor, and the two had been in discussion before the arrival of the detectives.

"Well, Anthony, do you know why you're here?"

"Give us a clue, love," he said, smirking broadly, and looking to the solicitor for approval of his wit.

Moore sat down alongside her colleague and continued.

"How do you know John McKenna, Anthony?"

"John who? I don't know no John McWhat-sit or whatever."

"Really. Are you quite sure, Anthony? It's important," Moore said.

"I told ye, I don't fucking know him. Are you thick or what?"

Moore was taking the measure of the man. She had interviewed many criminals in her past, and once she got on their wavelength, she could usually find a way to unlock whatever secrets they thought they were hiding.

"Why did you go to Manchester, Anthony?" Lawlor asked.

"A bit of a holiday. I got mates over there, haven't I?"

"What happened to your eye?" Moore asked.

"What's this, the bloody Morecambe and Wise show? Anyway, I walked into a door."

The interview went on in this vein for some time. O'Dowd had a smart answer for every question the detectives put to him, but in any case they were only warming him up for the main event when Burke joined the party.

They didn't have long to wait.

Burke came into the room and signalled to Lawlor that he would take over from him. He sat down noisily in the chair, scraping it across the concrete floor. He then leaned in close to the prisoner, breathing stale beer fumes right into his face.

"Look here, you little shite. As you may have guessed, I'm not in very good form this morning, and I'm not in the humour to put up with any of your nonsense. Now, we have a statement that says you attacked Emma Rowe in her apartment, and we have plenty of forensic evidence that places you at the scene too. So now you're going to tell me why you attacked her, or I might just have to take you downstairs and have a little one-on-one with you. Got it?"

"Inspector Burke, are you threatening my client?" the solicitor piped up.

"What the fuck do you think?" Burke snarled, glaring at the man who promptly shut up.

The room went quiet for a minute or two while Anto assessed the position.

"OK, I'll admit to slapping the girl about a bit. But that's all. I wasn't going to do anything real bad to her – just teach her a lesson like."

Fiona Moore withdrew a piece of paper from the file she had in front of her and passed it to Burke.

"'I've done your boyfriend, now it's your turn, you sad bitch'," Burke said. "Ring any bells?"

"No. I never said that to no one. Honest."

147

"So, what exactly did you say to Emma Rowe as you grabbed her round the mouth and tried to choke her?"

O'Dowd said nothing for a few minutes.

"I told you. I'll admit to giving her a slap, but that's it."

"I don't think so," Burke said and signalled to Moore that they were going to leave the room.

"Why don't we give you a few minutes to confer with your client, and remember, we have the girl's statement."

As they were getting up to leave, Moore tuned to O'Dowd and said, "By the way, where did you get the knife?"

"Knife, what knife? Jesus, what are you two on?"

The two detectives left the room.

When they got back up to Burke's office, he asked Moore to arrange more coffee for him, and when she had brought him a steaming mug of strong black Americano, he said to her, "We need some forensics from the knife they found in the bins. Have you checked?"

"Yes, of course. There was nothing. Just some anonymous prints, no blood other than the victim's. Nothing useful. Just that it seems to have been made in Russia."

"And how the hell does a low life like O'Dowd get caught up with Russian financiers. It doesn't make any sense. Get back on to forensics. Get them to go over it again. There must be something. We need a link to get the little shit to confess. Otherwise he's going to get eighteen months for assault, and I'm not having it. And there's something else. Why would Mr Anthony O'Dowd kill McKenna and have a go at his girlfriend? It's not like they moved in the same social circles after all. I want to find out what's behind it. Have we any clues on O'Dowd's known associates or even where he lives?"

"I think he was sleeping rough. But I'll get Dónal to check around, see what the uniform boys can tell us. And I'll check with forensics too. How long have we got?"

"All day today anyway, maybe longer."

"OK. Give me an hour."

"And while you're at it, see if anyone found any mobile phones anywhere. I can't believe one wasn't recovered – it doesn't feel right."

"Yes, I was thinking that too," Moore said, and left.

* * *

When she had briefed Dónal Lawlor, Moore called Jim in forensics.

"Hi, Jim. It's Fiona Moore here from Store Street. I'm just following up on that body we found in the lane at the back of Beresford Place, remember?"

"Yeah, sure. McKenna wasn't it?"

"Yes, that's the one. Inspector Burke is going mad. He wants to know if there were any traces on the knife, or any other forensic evidence that could help to identify the killer? And he's asking about mobile phones too. Was anything like that found?"

"Hang on. Let me have a look. Hold on a minute."

He was back a couple of minutes later.

"Sergeant Moore, did you not get the information about the phone?"

"No, what phone?"

"There was a phone found in the drain near the body. It's pretty dirty, but I have it here. I thought Julie sent you an email about it."

"Jesus, Jim. Whose phone was it?"

"McKenna's, I think. At least his fingerprints were all over it. Look, I can get it sent over to you if you like. The battery is flat, so I don't know if it's working or not, but it may be some use."

"Yeah, would you? Quick as you like, Jim. It could be important."

When Moore was finished with Jim, she called Jane Langford and asked what she could do with a phone that had been found in a drain and had a flat battery.

"If the SIM card is still in it, and it isn't damaged, we should be able to get something from it. And we can get the phone records from the airtime provider," Langford said.

"Any chance you could come down? I'll have it here in about half an hour."

"Yeah, sure. See you soon."

Moore told Burke about the new developments which cheered him up a good deal.

"Let's wait to talk to Anto again till we see what new evidence we can get from the phone. It might give us a clue as to what the bloody hell is going on."

Chapter Twenty-Six

Jane Langford took the tiny SIM card out of what had once been John McKenna's phone and dried it off carefully. She then took a pencil rubber and stroked the gold contacts on the tiny card, inserting it into another phone that she had with her.

After a few moments, she had activated the instrument, and was restoring all the data that McKenna's phone had backed up to the cloud.

Moore came over to where Langford was working.

"Anything?" she asked.

"Yep! Just getting it loaded up now. There are text messages and emails on here that may have something in them," Langford said.

"Great. Can I have a look?"

"Hang on a mo. Here you go."

Moore took the host phone and started to scroll down through the messages that John McKenna had received before his death. Many of them were from Emma Rowe, and several of them complained about calls and messages she had received from her ex-boyfriend, Derek Cotter. At one stage, she had messaged McKenna to say that she was getting scared of him, and asked what she should do.

McKenna had tried to reassure her that it was all hot air, but it was clear that Cotter had a nasty streak, and it was getting to Emma.

"Can you get these printed out for us, Jane? They could be important."

"Yes, sure. Catch you later."

Moore went to find Burke and update him with the latest information.

"For fuck sake. How come those numpties in forensics didn't inform us. Sometimes this place really sucks. On the subject of phones, did our boy O'Dowd have one on him when he came in?"

"Yes, I think so. The desk sergeant will have it."

"Well, get it, will you? And give it to Langford as well and see if she can get anything useful off it."

"Righto, I'm on it."

* * *

There wasn't much of any value to be found on O'Dowd's phone. He kept it more or less clean, apart from a few entries in the contacts list, and one or two recent messages between himself and his friends from Manchester about his flight home. The phone was connected to the Worldfone network, an overseas company that largely supplied airtime to foreigners in Ireland. Needless to say, it wasn't registered – a 'burner', as the Garda called it.

"Any luck with O'Dowd's phone, Jane?" Moore said.

"It's one of those pesky Worldfone jobs. I've come across these before. The company is based somewhere ending in -istan. They're not very helpful, but I can try and get the records from them."

"When it connects up to the local masts here, does someone not keep records locally?"

"Not a chance – too much traffic for that. But I'll get onto them and see what I can shake loose. You never know."

"Please. It could be important."

Moore went back to Burke's office and told him the news.

"Right. Well, let's get back in there with O'Dowd and see if we can open him up a bit. Just follow my lead. I might have to be a tad unconventional for this one."

When they got back to the interview room, O'Dowd was still playing it super cool. Burke decided it was time for a little special treatment.

"Right, O'Dowd. Here is where we are with this. We have you banged to rights for the assault on the girl, and you condemned yourself with your very own words concerning the murder of John McKenna, so you're looking at a lifer one way or the other," Burke said.

O'Dowd's solicitor felt the need to demonstrate that he was earning his keep.

"Inspector, you know very well that your so-called evidence won't hold up. It's very flimsy. My client has admitted to a mild assault on Emma Rowe. So, why don't we leave it at that? Charge him and bail him."

"OK. I hear you. But, you see, it's not quite as simple as that. We know about the Russian connection, and the courts won't take kindly when we tell them that your client here was acting on instructions from a foreign power. Of course, neither will the Russians. I'd say things could get a bit tricky for Mr O'Dowd around these parts, wouldn't you? Those boys have all sorts of interesting ways of dealing with the likes of you. Remember Salisbury – very unpleasant," Burke said.

Moore couldn't quite believe what she was hearing, but stayed quiet.

"Look here. How many times do I have to tell you, I don't know nothing about no fucking Russians! Bleeding hell – where are you getting all this shite from?"

Burke said nothing and just stared at O'Dowd.

"Look, Anto, you really need to start telling us what all this is about. I'm not messing here – your life could be in real danger. Whatever we do to you will be chicken feed compared to that other lot. If I were you, I'd come clean," Moore said.

"May I have a few minutes to confer with my client, Inspector?"

"Certainly. Say, thirty minutes. Can we get you some refreshment? Tea? Coffee? Water?"

"Coffee would be fine, thanks," the man said.

Outside the interview room, Burke said to Moore, "The old good cop bad cop routine – never fails."

"We'll see. This better give us something. We've got bugger all without some kind of revelation from O'Dowd."

"Anything from the phones?" Burke said.

"It's not looking good. Except that guy Cotter seems to have been getting a bit nasty towards Emma."

"Hmm. I doubt if that's anything to do with this mess, though. My money is on the Ruskies."

* * *

Jane Langford had spent almost an hour on the phone to the Worldfone head office. At first she was passed from one customer service agent to another, none of whom spoke good English, until eventually she managed to persuade one of them to hand her over to a manager.

After a bit of coming and going with this woman, Langford convinced her that she wouldn't be breaking any international treaties if she just sent across the records from O'Dowd's phone, and after a bit more discussion, she agreed to do just that.

The information arrived in Langford's inbox several minutes later. It was a mixture of sound recordings in a format that Langford had never seen before, and text messages going back three months. The Worldfone woman had explained that they only keep records for that length of time, as otherwise they would be overwhelmed with material.

Langford searched the web for a programme or application that could decipher the sound messages, and found one which she was able to download, hoping that it wasn't packed with viruses.

When she finally got to listen to the conversations, she was intrigued. She couldn't wait to tell the detectives what she had learnt.

Jane Langford caught the two of them just as they were going back down for the next round of questioning with O'Dowd. She explained what she had discovered from his phone, and told them that she was now going to get to work on McKenna's phone and see if she could correlate anything.

"How long will that take, Jane?" Moore asked.

"I'll need another hour, at least. Is that a problem?"

"No. We can leave him to stew for a while longer if you think it would be worth it."

"Well, it looks as if we may be able to get something from it. I'll be as quick as I can."

"OK. Thanks."

* * *

Just over an hour later, Jane Langford was back in Burke's office with all that she had recovered from the two phones.

Burke and Moore studied the printouts carefully.

"Right. Let's get back in there. This should be fun!" Burke said. He was beginning to feel better already.

Chapter Twenty-Seven

"Well, Anto. We now have evidence to show that you were hired by person or persons unknown to 'deal with' John McKenna and his girlfriend Emma Rowe. What we need you to tell us, Anto, is who hired you." Burke said.

O'Dowd looked at his solicitor, who remained stony-faced.

"I don't know," O'Dowd said after a minute or two.

"You don't know what, Anto?" Moore said.

"I don't know who the fecker was. He just called me. Never gave a name. Promised me a monkey to deal with them, and told me where McKenna would be that night. I didn't mean to kill him though. That wasn't supposed to happen."

"I see. So, you admit to stabbing John McKenna in the lane at the back of Beresford Place then, Anto?" Moore said.

Anto gave his solicitor another furtive look.

"I guess. And I never got me bleeding money neither. Scum bag!"

"And who exactly was it that asked you to do this?"

"I dunno. Some geezer on the phone. Me mate Charlo said he was sound."

"Are you seriously expecting us to believe that you were going to kill two people that you didn't know on the basis of a phone call from someone else that you'd never met on the promise of five hundred euro?"

"That's about it, yeah." O'Dowd didn't want to reveal that he had in fact met Derek Cotter. The less the police knew about it, the better.

"Did you speak to this anonymous person? Did he have a foreign accent?" Burke said.

"No he fucking didn't. And yes, I spoke to him..."

"Did this Charlie guy know him?" Moore asked.

"Yeah, I think so. I heard him talking to him on the phone a couple of times. He called him Dekko, I think."

O'Dowd's solicitor spoke up again.

"Inspector, are you going to charge my client? It's getting late, and I have to be somewhere."

"All in good time. We need to check out a few things first. We'll be back in a few minutes," Burke said.

When they got back to Burke's office, there was a message for him to call Edmund Giltrap with a mobile number.

Burke looked at the Post-it Note, and said, "I'll deal with that later. So, looks like this fella Cotter may be our man after all, and there we were chasing all over the shop after some mythical Russians. Typical!"

"Well, boss, I did try to tell you that Cotter could be of interest," Moore said.

"Hmm, OK, no need to rub it in. Any ideas?"

"Yes. I have, actually. We don't know where Cotter is, but maybe we could use O'Dowd to flush him out in the open. What do you think?"

"Perhaps. What have you got in mind?"

Moore went on to outline her plan, and while Burke thought it was a bit risky, he agreed that it was probably worth giving it a go, but he had reservations.

"I don't know, Fiona. We have O'Dowd for the murder now, is that not enough for you?"

"Yes, but if this guy Cotter commissioned the killings, we need to put him away too. God knows what he'll get up to next."

"Maybe. Let's see."

The two detectives went back down to the interview room.

* * *

"Right, Anthony, we're just about ready to charge you with murder and assault with intent now, but just before we do, there are some loose ends we'd like to tie up."

Moore outlined her plan, and O'Dowd listened intently.

"And what will I get out of this?" he said when he had heard what she had to say.

"We'll see. We could perhaps reduce the charge to manslaughter, if you can convince us that you didn't actually intend to kill McKenna. That will probably get you eight years instead of fifteen."

"I didn't mean to kill him, honest. I'm not used to handling blades," O'Dowd said reassuringly.

"Where did you get the knife anyway?" Moore asked.

"Some dude in the pub had it. Said it was Russian Army issue. He only wanted twenty euro for it. I should have left it alone."

"And when exactly do you want my client to assist you with this operation, Inspector?" the solicitor asked.

"Let's keep him here overnight, and then we'll try tomorrow and see how we get on. If all goes well, we could have it all tied up by tomorrow evening," Burke said.

"And will you bail my client?"

"If we get what we want, we won't oppose bail."

"Right. Well, I'll be off so. See you in court," the solicitor said packing away his few papers hurriedly.

* * *

The following morning, Jane Langford had set up all sorts of electronics on the desk in Burke's room.

Everything that took place would be carefully recorded. While this was going on, Burke and Moore had coached Anthony O'Dowd with exactly how to play the phone conversation with Derek Cotter.

"Remember, seven years of freedom relies on you getting this just right, Anthony," she said when O'Dowd was brought up from the cells to participate in the Gardaí's sting operation.

O'Dowd sat down and picked up his mobile phone. He dialled the number that Langford had retrieved from his phone earlier, and after two rings it was answered.

"Who's this?" The person on the other end of the call was quite well spoken, but seemed to be surprised at getting a call on this particular phone.

"How are ye, Dekko, me old pal. This is Anto here."

"What the fuck do you want?"

"Ah, now, Dekko, that's no way to talk to a mate. What I want is me money. Remember the five hundred euro you owe me?"

"I don't owe you five hundred. You never finished the job. I had to take care of the silly cow myself. And I never agreed to pay for half a job."

Burke and Moore looked at each other with surprise. So, it was Cotter who had attacked Emma Rowe that night down by the river; broken her neck, and thrown her over the low quayside wall.

"All the same," Anto went on unperturbed, "you owe me at least two fifty, and I mean to collect, one way or the other."

Cotter remained silent for a few minutes processing his options. He didn't want to fall completely foul of this thug. It might not end well for him, and he knew O'Dowd could handle a knife.

"Okay. Two fifty. Where? When?"

"Meet me in the ILAC car park. Third floor, near the lift, tonight at eleven. And no messing. Come alone and bring the dosh. No tricks, or you'll be sorry." He hung up.

The ILAC was a shopping centre in the middle of Dublin that had a large car park attached opening onto Parnell Street. At eleven at night it would be pretty well deserted, so it was a good venue for what was to come.

"Well done, Anto. Right, let's get the arrangements made."

Chapter Twenty-Eight

"Are you going to tell the Super, boss? Get the troops out?" Moore said.

"Ah, no. Sure there's no need. We should be able to handle an office worker all by ourselves, don't you think? Or are you afraid he's going to attack you with his stapler?" Burke smirked.

"No, course not. But it looks as if he killed his ex-girlfriend, and he may have something lined up for Anthony. It might be better to be a little prepared," Moore said.

"Away with ye. He's hardly the most sophisticated of criminals now, is he? But if you're feeling queasy about it, why not draw a weapon? Just don't feckin shoot me with the bloody thing, OK?"

Moore wasn't expecting such a harsh put down from her boss. But she let it slide, given that he was probably hungover. But she just might take his advice and draw a gun from the armoury. She had been fully firearms trained some time ago, and her certificate was right up to date.

They put O'Dowd back down in the cells for the day as they prepared for the evening's rendezvous.

Burke got together with Fiona Moore and Dónal Lawlor to sketch out their plan.

"Right. We'll drop O'Dowd off at the end of the street in case Cotter is watching," Burke said. Fiona Moore immediately put up her hand.

"Do you not think he might abscond, boss?"

"It's a chance we'll have to take. We can't exactly deliver him in a shiny new squad car, can we? Anyway, I'll be having a word with Mr O'Dowd before the off, and I think I'll be able to persuade him not to be stupid."

Moore looked at Lawlor, who was thinking the same thing.

"We'll position three cars on the third floor: one near the exit ramp; one near the pedestrian stairs; and the other right out in the open in the middle of the area. O'Dowd will be lounging against the outside wall of the car park, close to the third car, and when Cotter shows up, and they get close to each other, I'll jump out and take him down. If he gets away from me, you two act as backup and make sure we capture him."

It was Dónal Lawlor's turn to interrupt.

"What about O'Dowd?"

"Don't worry about Anto. By the time I've finished with him, he'll be begging to get back into Garda custody," Burke said.

"Boss, I'm really not happy about all of this. I think we need more resources on it. Can we not at least position some officers at the exit from the car park in case it all goes pear-shaped?" Moore said.

"Very well, but you'll have to justify the extra expense to the Super if he queries it. I've told him it's just a straightforward lift of a suspect."

Moore wasn't happy. She knew Burke was inclined to be a bit of a maverick, but they had no measure of this Cotter bloke, except that he was a nasty piece of work. Anything could happen.

"Right then. We'll meet here at nine o'clock tonight," Burke said.

When the team had dispersed, Burke said to Moore, "I have to ring Giltrap, he was looking for me."

"OK, I'll leave you to it then."

* * *

"Edmund Giltrap."

"Hello, Mr Giltrap. It's Inspector Burke here. You were looking for me."

"Oh, yes, thank you, Inspector. Look, there have been some developments concerning John McKenna that I wanted to talk to you about. Firstly, you should know that I have been let go from the bank. But as far as you are concerned, that's not a bad thing, because now I can speak more openly to you about what's been going on."

"I see. Well, I'm sorry to hear you have lost your job. I hope it wasn't our fault," Burke said.

"Oh, no, nothing like that. And I got a good settlement from them, so it may work out all for the best in any case. I was getting a bit fed up with it to be truthful. But I was wondering if we could meet for a chat?"

"Yes, sure. When suits?"

"Would today at lunch time be good for you?"

"OK. What about that new hotel on the south side of the river just by the Millennium Bridge?"

"Yes, that will be fine. Can we say one o'clock?"

"Perfect. See you there."

"That was Giltrap," Burke said to Moore as she entered the room, "He wants to meet. He's been chucked out of the bank. Says he has some more information for us about McKenna."

"I see. Are you going to meet him?" Moore said.

"Yes, I am, at lunch time."

"Do you want me to tag along?"

"No, I don't think so, not today. I got the impression he'd open up more if it was kinda informal, so I'll go on my own," Burke said.

"OK, whatever. Don't forget to come back though – we need to fix things up for tonight."

"As if!"

* * *

When Aidan Burke arrived at the hotel at five past one, Giltrap was already seated at a low table looking out onto the busy street.

"Inspector. Can I get you something?"

"A pint of Guinness, thanks."

Giltrap signalled to the lounge girl and placed the order. He was drinking sparkling water.

"So, what's this new information you have for me then?" Burke asked.

"It's about that chap Zanuk and his investment firm, Hastavia," Giltrap said, moving in closer to Burke and looking around in case anyone might overhear them.

"He's been here before. I know he put up a good show in front of our auditors, but that's not the whole story. That was just to see if he could get compensation, which he will do, of course."

"I see. So, what is the whole story, Mr Giltrap?"

"Zanuk knew all about what John McKenna was doing. McKenna was up to other tricks as well that were to Hastavia's benefit."

"What sort of tricks?"

"Dodging round various regulations and limits that the bank has for foreign investments. Avoiding some of the statutory reporting we're supposed to do. Manipulating dates on transactions to benefit Hastavia, that sort of thing."

"And would Zanuk have made much out of these 'tricks' as you call them?"

"Yes, definitely. When you're dealing with very large sums of money, even a tenth of a percent makes a huge difference."

"And what was your role in all of this?"

"I just turned a blind eye. I might have signed off on some of the stuff that needed a manager's signature too, once or twice."

"I see, so basically, you were up to your neck in it."

Giltrap shifted uneasily in his seat and looked down at the table. He stayed quiet as the lounge girl returned with Burke's pint of stout.

"How did you come across this guy, anyway?" Burke said, wiping the cream off his upper lip.

"A broker called Cotter introduced him to us. His firm was too small to handle the huge amounts that Zanuk was dealing in, and they didn't have the FX capability either, so he introduced Hastavia to the bank. They got a nice slice of commission from it too, I can tell you."

"Would that be Derek Cotter?"

"Yes. He works for a place out in Blackrock. Small outfit."

"But we asked you previously if you knew anyone by that name, and you said no."

"I know. I'm sorry. I was lying. I didn't want to get involved."

"So, why are you telling me all this now then?"

"Isn't it obvious? I may need protection. These aren't the types you mess with, and two people who knew what was going on have been killed already, and I have a wife and family, you know," Giltrap said. He was becoming a little more animated at the thought of what might become of him.

"That's not going to happen, Mr Giltrap. We have bigger things to be doing than running around after some corrupt philandering bank manager. You'll be fine. Let me know if you get any direct threats."

Burke drained his pint, put the glass down on the table, got up, and left.

Chapter Twenty-Nine

"All set then?" Burke said as he addressed the small team at ten minutes to nine. It was a really awful evening in Dublin, with hard persistent rain falling that showed no signs of letting up.

"Boss. I hope you don't mind, but I've arranged a few more plain clothes officers to be dotted around the car park while this is going down. They'll stay well out of the way unless we need them."

"Whatever," Burke said dismissively.

The desk sergeant brought Anthony O'Dowd up from the cells.

"Right, Anto. All you have to do is stand over by the car park wall where we said and wait for Cotter to approach. You don't even have to say anything, leave the rest to us, OK?" Burke said.

"Yeah, right. And when you have him, you'll reduce the charges against me, right?" O'Dowd was very distrustful, especially of the Gardaí, but he didn't have much of a choice in this instance.

"Don't worry, Anthony, it will be fine," Moore said.

They arrived at the car park soon after nine and set the cars up as arranged. They had one radio check with all three vehicles and the men that Moore had positioned down on the street. They then settled in for a long wait.

Every few minutes someone would come onto the third floor to retrieve their car and set off home. The Gardaí watched intently, but most of the shoppers had one or more large paper bags with them, so they were clearly of no interest.

By ten forty-five the place had thinned out almost entirely. The shops closed at nine, so once the shoppers and the staff had left, there were just a few other vehicles remaining, probably belonging to guests who were staying over in one of the many hotels in the area.

"Right, Anto. Out you get. And don't think you can just run off. We have the place well covered, and if you try to scarper, all bets are off," Moore said.

O'Dowd got out of the car and strolled slowly over to the spot that had been pointed out to him earlier, lounging casually against the outer wall of the car park. From their vantage point, Moore, Burke and Lawlor all had him in sight, and with the place now nearly deserted, they could see the pedestrian entrance and vehicle ramp clearly as well.

At five past eleven, the door from the stairs opened and a man came through onto the floor. He looked around cautiously, and seeing nothing to alarm him, started walking over to where O'Dowd was still stationed by the wall. As Cotter approached him, O'Dowd said, "How are ya Dekko, got me dosh?"

"I have it here for you," Cotter replied, reaching into the pocket of his jacket. He was now only a few metres from O'Dowd.

The next thing the Gardaí heard was O'Dowd screaming "For fuck sake!" followed rapidly by the unmistakeable crack of a small pistol going off. O'Dowd grabbed his stomach as a second shot found his head, and he went down hard. By the time he had reached the cold wet concrete, he was dead.

The Gardaí scrambled to get out of their cars. Moore was the only one that was armed, and it took her a few split seconds to open the door, clamber out and retrieve her Sig Sauer pistol from her belt. By the time she was ready to use it, Cotter had departed via the stairs again.

The Gardaí gave chase having little regard for their own safety. Cotter was quick. He descended the stairs two at a time till he was on the first floor. Then he ran out onto the car park itself, across the concourse, and leapt out over the wall at the other side just as the Gardaí were entering.

Moore got on her radio to the men she had positioned close to the vehicular entrance to the car park.

"Suspect on the run. He's gone over the wall from the first floor into the lane. He's armed, so extreme caution."

Burke was on his phone summoning an ambulance for the beleaguered O'Dowd, but he knew instinctively that it was too late. The lad was past saving.

"Shit, shit, shit," he shouted out loud, as he stood over the prone form of the victim. "Why didn't I listen to Moore? Fuck it!" he said to himself.

The Gardaí who had been positioned down on the street ran to the lane at the side of the car park where Cotter had presumably landed after his acrobatics. There was no sign. They searched around for half an hour or so, questioned a few people that they encountered coming and going through the narrow streets, but no one had seen anything, and Cotter had got clean away.

Burke stayed with O'Dowd until the ambulance came and removed the body. He then called forensics to get them out to examine the scene in case Cotter had left any evidence behind him, although he wasn't hopeful. It had been a clean kill, and a very ruthless one at that.

While he was waiting, he put out a general call for the suspect, again warning his colleagues to approach with extreme caution. At this point, Cotter had very little to lose by shooting anyone who came near him.

At just after midnight, Burke got on the radio again and called everyone back to the station for a debrief.

* * *

The mood at Store Street was very solemn. The operation had been a total disaster. Moore tried to reassure Burke that it wasn't really his fault.

"Unless we had swamped the place with men, there was nothing we could do. And if we had done that, Cotter would have smelled a rat and taken off. So, it wasn't your fault."

"Still, it's my name all over it. Heffernan will go ape. But wait – we might be able to rescue something from this mess if we act quickly. I'm going to call Edmund Giltrap."

Burke took out his phone and dialled Giltrap's number. It was answered after three rings by a very sleepy voice that just said, "Hello."

"Mr Giltrap, this is Inspector Burke. Sorry to call you at this hour, but there have been some developments and we need some information urgently."

"Oh. OK," Giltrap replied.

"This Derek Cotter guy. Have you any idea where he lives?"

"Me. No, why should I? But wait a minute, I think I did hear him say, or maybe it was McKenna who said it, that he thought Cotter lived with his sister somewhere in Phibsboro, at least I think that's where it was."

"Do you know if the sister is married?"

"Haven't a clue, sorry. Now can I get back to sleep?"

"Yes, thanks. Sorry for disturbing you."

When Burke was off the phone, he turned to Moore.

"See if you can find a Cotter living in Phibsboro – a woman. It's a bit of a long shot, but Giltrap thinks Derek Cotter may be living there with his sister."

"OK, I'll see if we can find anything."

Moore went off to scour the Gardaí computers to see if there was any trace of a Cotter in that area, while Burke searched his desk in vain for some whiskey. All he found was a bottle of Jameson with nothing but the dregs left in it.

While Moore was looking for Cotter's address, Burke tried to make sense of the web of names and contacts that they had detected concerning the death of John McKenna. He drew circles on his jotter and wrote McKenna, Rowe, Giltrap, Zanuk, O'Dowd and Cotter into each one and then tried to connect them with lines. But after a few minutes, he gave up. None of it made any sense. He could see some connections clearly, but not enough to provide a motive for three murders.

He went in search of some strong coffee.

* * *

Moore came back into his office looking triumphant and carrying a piece of paper.

"There ya go. Aileen Cotter, 14 O'Boyle Road, Phibsboro," she said waving the piece of paper around.

"Fuck me. How did you get that so quickly?" Burke said.

"Easy. She has a vehicle registered at that address. A Toyota Yaris. Road Tax is even up to date."

"God, well done, Fiona. Right. Let's see if our man is at home."

"What, now?"

"No. We'll go in at about four-thirty, and this time we'll bring the Armed Response Unit with us. What's the geography of O'Boyle Road like?"

"Here. Let's bring it up on Google Maps," Moore said, and wriggled the mouse on Burke's PC to wake it up.

"See, here it is. Looks like it's a cul-de-sac with a lane running behind it. There's about twenty houses along its length in all."

"Perfect. We can box him in nicely. What's that at the end of the road, look where it finishes."

Moore fiddled with the computer some more and brought up Street View for O'Boyle Road.

"It looks like the wall of a factory, or warehouse. It's solid anyway."

"Good. No chance Spiderman will get away this time then. Nice work, Sergeant. Now can you get the troops organised. I need some kip, so close the door on your way out."

Chapter Thirty

The rain had eased off considerably by three-thirty in the morning when the Gardaí began to organise themselves in Phibsboro. There was very little traffic about – mostly just taxis driven by Indians and Africans taking well-oiled fares home to sleep it off.

They positioned two ARU officers in the lane behind number fourteen, one either side of the wooden door from the back of the house. They had a jeep parked across the entrance to the lane too, and more ARU officers were waiting in it, ready to move in the event that Cotter managed to get past their two colleagues.

At the main entrance to O'Boyle Road, two unmarked Garda cars were positioned in a V formation so that if Cotter tried to ram them in his sister's car, he wouldn't get very far. More ARU officers were positioned up along the road, with two of them beyond number fourteen, primed for action.

"OK. You know the drill. Bang like fuck on the door, and if it isn't answered within ten seconds, then bash it down. Let's make sure the bugger knows we're coming for him. And if you see a weapon, shoot first. I don't want to lose anyone else tonight at this fecker's hands," Burke said.

The men walked up the street to number fourteen where, obligingly, the number was screwed to the front door in polished brass figures.

Burke gave the nod.

They were just getting ready to smash the door in when a light came on in the hallway. A moment later, the door was opened by a barefoot girl in a long T-shirt and tousled brown hair rubbing the sleep from her eyes.

Burke took her by the elbow and ushered her out onto the damp footpath while three uniformed Gardaí, all armed, piled into the little house.

"What's going on?" the girl asked.

"It's all right, love. It's Derek we're after. Is he in?" Burke said.

"Yeah, 'course. He's asleep. But what's he done?"

Their conversation was interrupted by two of the Gardaí dragging a very dejected looking Derek Cotter out from the hall, dressed just in boxer shorts. When he was standing before Aidan Burke, Burke told him he was arresting him for the murder of Anthony O'Dowd and cited the rest of the mantra for such occasions.

"Right lads, take him away."

Burke turned to Cotter's sister, "He's only shot someone dead, that's all. Now we need to find the gun, so you won't mind if we come in and have a look round, will you?"

The girl dissolved into tears, bowing her head, but she didn't try to impede the Gardaí from re-entering her house.

"Whatever you find, lads, bring it back to the station. And bring along his laptop and his phone as well, and don't forget whatever clothes he was wearing tonight."

* * *

When Cotter arrived at Store Street Garda station, Moore arranged for a forensic officer to take swabs from Cotter's hands and wrists to collect any blowback residue from the gun he had used. He was also fingerprinted, and a DNA sample was collected from inside his mouth. His clothes were handed over too, and he was put into a one-piece jump suit and escorted to a cell for the remainder of the night.

Moore said to the night man, "Keep a good eye on him for me now. We'll interview him at around midday when the forensic teams have finished at his house."

"Ah, don't worry, Fiona, he's in good hands," the sergeant said.

* * *

Burke and Moore went home to get a few hours' sleep before sitting down with Derek Cotter and, no doubt, his appointed solicitor to interview him. During the early hours, the forensic team returned to the station. They had found the gun that Cotter had stashed in his bedside locker, and they had his mobile phone and laptop too.

Moore arrived in at eleven and started to prepare for the interview. Burke arrived soon after her, and they got together for a chat before starting in on their suspect.

"So, what have we got from forensics, Fiona?" Burke asked.

"Lots. They collected two spent shell casings from the car park. They haven't dug the bullets out of O'Dowd yet, but I don't think we'll need them. Cotter has gunpowder residue on his right hand, and there are two bullets missing from the magazine in the gun. And don't forget, three Gardaí saw him shoot O'Dowd as well. I'd say he's banged to rights."

"That's all well and good, but I want to know why. So far all we have is all sorts of shite involving some Bulgarian and a few bankers. I want to know what the hell went down here, and if there's anyone else at risk, so I'm going to go in fairly hard on Mr Cotter."

Moore assembled a few pages into a manila folder, and the two detectives set off to start work on their suspect.

"Right, Cotter, now listen to me. We're obviously going to charge you with the murder of Anthony O'Dowd. But before we do, I want to know what this is all about. So, let's hear your story."

"No comment," came the reply from Derek Cotter.

"I see. Well, play it that way if you like, Cotter, but I'm telling you, it's not very smart. You're already going down for life for murder, and I'm quite convinced you had a good bit to do with the death of two other victims as well. And what's all this with this Bulgarian bloke – Zanuk?"

"I have no idea what you're talking about. I suppose you're just going to fit me up for a couple of unsolved cases now that you have me here," Cotter said.

"That's not my style, Cotter. But hear this. If you force me to spend weeks and weeks carrying out further investigations to get to the bottom of whatever has been going on, let's just say, it won't go well for you. Understand?"

"Do what you like, I don't care," Cotter said.

Burke nodded to Moore, and they got up and left the room.

As they walked back up to the office, Moore said, "Give me a few minutes to check something out, will you? I have an idea."

"Are you going to tell me what it is?"

"Ah, it's probably nothing. I'll be back shortly." She went off towards the evidence room.

Burke got a coffee and spent a few minutes quietly thinking over the case in his own office. He still couldn't join the dots to see what the whole thing was about. Maybe they would just charge Cotter with O'Dowd's murder and leave it at that. They could put McKenna's murder down to O'Dowd, but that left the killing of Emma Rowe outstanding.

"Still, two out of three isn't bad," he said to himself, but he wasn't happy.

Moore came in carrying a plastic evidence bag.

"What have you there, Fiona?"

"It's the knife that was used on McKenna, and guess what. That print that we couldn't identify – well, it's only Cotter's, isn't it?"

"Shit. Are you serious? Christ, this bloody case is hurting my head. So, it could be Cotter's blade?" Burke said.

"Hmm… maybe, or maybe not. But it ties him to McKenna's murder too, doesn't it?"

"Yes, and with the other evidence – what Anto told us about the five hundred euro. It looks as if Cotter hired O'Dowd to kill McKenna and his girlfriend, but why? Surely he wasn't just pissed off because she rejected him?"

"Let's go and have another chat with our hero, and see what he has to say for himself now then."

Back in the interview room, Moore produced the knife, still in its plastic evidence bag.

"Have you ever seen this weapon before, Derek?" she asked.

"No. Where did you get that then?"

"It's the knife that was used to kill John McKenna," Moore said.

"I've never seen it before, honest."

"That's odd. So, how do you account for the fact that there's your fingerprint on it?"

Cotter turned to his solicitor, who frankly had seemed totally disinterested in the proceedings from the start.

"See – I told you they'd fit me up, didn't I? This is crazy."

Moore pulled her chair in close to the table and looked Cotter straight in the face.

"Now, see here, Derek. This blade ties you directly to the murder of John McKenna. And we have the phone call where you admitted to Anthony O'Dowd that you 'took care' of Emma Rowe yourself. That's on top of the cold-blooded killing of O'Dowd that we witnessed in the car park. But if we were to find that you were acting for another party, say under duress of some kind, then things might go a bit differently for you."

Finally, the solicitor perked up and said, "I wonder if I could have a few minutes to confer with my client, Inspector?"

"Yes, certainly. Shall we say fifteen minutes?" Burke and Moore got up and left the room.

"Nice one, Fiona. So, who do you think might be behind all these killings?"

"Let's see what he says. But you'll have to excuse me for a minute or two, I have something to do."

"OK. See you in quarter of an hour," Burke said.

* * *

"My client would like to make a statement, Inspector. You were right of course, he was acting under duress when he set these, eh, incidents up, leading to the unfortunate death of Mr McKenna and Ms Rowe. He was in fear for his life at the time, and he now regrets his actions very sincerely."

"Is he willing to tell us the whole story?" Burke said.

"Yes, he is, but we would like to know first what the Garda attitude towards his involvement would be," the solicitor said.

"We can't make any promises, but if we get the full story, and it enables us to close these various cases, we'll see what we can do."

"Hmm... right. I trust you will be reasonable, Inspector."

The solicitor nodded to his client.

"OK. Well, this is all down to that Bulgarian guy, Zanuk. He was working with my company, but we couldn't do the kind of things he wanted us to do, so I introduced him to the National. But after a while, things started to go wrong, and he got spooked, thinking McKenna might blow the whistle on the whole operation. So he came over, and we met. He offered me ten grand to deal with McKenna and his girlfriend. I knew her from before – we'd been out together a bit a while back. He gave me the knife. He said it was his grandfather's. Apparently he was in the Russian army and fought on the front line during the Second World War."

"So, what did you do?" Moore asked.

"Well, I didn't fancy doing it myself. I'm not into that kind of thing at all. I wouldn't know how to go about it. But I knew if I went down to that shit-hole of a pub behind Sherriff Street, I'd find some patsy to do the job for me. And I wasn't wrong. It took a few visits, but I got chatting to Anto, and he took on the job for five hundred. No bother. It was handy. I'd be quids in, McKenna and Rowe would be taken care of, and Zanuk would be happy. Except he made an arse of it, didn't he?"

"I see. But that doesn't sound like duress to me. Where does that come in?" Burke said.

"Zanuk. He told me that he was paying well for the job to be done, and if anything went wrong, he'd be back to see me personally, and it wouldn't end well for me."

"And that's what you call duress?"

"You know what these Eastern Europeans are like – you don't mess with them."

"What about the knife?" Moore asked.

"He gave it to me and said he wanted the job to be done using it. For ten grand, I didn't argue – would you?"

"So, what about Emma Rowe?" Burke asked.

"When Anto made a bags of killing her, I had to deal with it myself. It was easy. I met her at the train station and we went for a coffee, for old time's sake. I apologised for being an asshole, and she accepted it. I was being ever so charming, and we got on really well. Then we were walking back towards the station, and I just grabbed her and twisted her head around till I heard it snap, then pushed her over the wall. There was no one about. I was lucky."

"Unlike poor Emma Rowe," Moore said.

"She knew too much. McKenna and her were in it together. Zanuk was paying him on the side to do dodgy deals for him, and he was at it himself too. If it came out, Hastavia would be ruined."

"OK. Well, we need to get all of this written down. I'll leave you to do that, and then we'll see where we go from here. I'll be back in an hour or so," Burke said.

Burke went in search of Fiona Moore and found her in the open plan office at her desk. He briefly described what had taken place during the interview with Cotter.

"If only we had this Zanuk character, we could wrap the whole thing up in a nice pink bow and be done with it all," Burke said.

"We have. He's on his way back in from the airport in a squad car now."

"What? How the hell did you manage that?"

"Easy. I figured he'd be leaving town, and there's only one way out of here to Bulgaria, so I got the guys out at the airport to lift him," Moore said with a satisfied smile on her face.

"Nice one! We'd better make sure to keep him well away from Cotter till we question him though."

"I agree. He's going to Pearse Street station – just in case. Why don't we walk around there and have a nice little chat. I'll bring the knife with me to help his memory."

Chapter Thirty-One

"Well, Mr Zanuk. I'm glad you didn't leave without talking to us," Burke said as they sat down opposite the man in the interview room at Pearse Garda station.

"You can't do this to me. I'm a European citizen. I have rights, you know, and I have done nothing illegal."

"Well now, Gregor, that's not strictly speaking true, is it? Apart altogether from your rather strange financial dealings, there's the matter of John McKenna's murder – and that of his girlfriend."

"That was very tragic, but nothing whatever to do with me, I can assure you," Zanuk said.

On cue, Moore lifted up the evidence bag containing the knife that had been used to kill McKenna and placed it on the table.

"Have you ever seen this before, Mr Zanuk?"

Zanuk held the bag containing the weapon and looked at it sombrely for a moment. The detectives thought they could see tears forming in his eyes. He dropped the knife back on the table, and looking away, said, "No comment."

"You see, Mr Zanuk, we have…"

The door to the interview room opened and a uniformed Garda leant over Burke and whispered something in his ear.

"I'm sorry, folks, I need a moment," Burke said, and signalled Moore to join him outside.

"Heffernan wants me – in person. Says it's urgent. Can you hold the fort here till I get back?"

"Yeah, sure. I'll postpone the interview for an hour or so. Will that be enough?" Moore said.

"Should be. I'll call you if I'm going to be any longer."

Moore went back into the interview room.

"Look here, officer. Not only have you detained me here on a false premise, but now I have missed my plane back to Sofia. I must insist you release me immediately. This is outrageous!" Zanuk shouted.

"We won't keep you any longer than necessary, Mr Zanuk. Would you like me to arrange a solicitor for you?"

"Damn you. NO. I don't want a lawyer, all I want is to get out of here."

"Settle down, sir. No one is going anywhere for at least another hour. Now, perhaps a cup of tea or coffee would help you to relax?" Moore said.

Zanuk did not reply.

Outside Pearse Street Garda station, a sleek black Mercedes limousine with darkened windows glided to a halt and stopped on the double yellow lines.

* * *

"Come in, Aidan, take a seat," Superintendent Heffernan said, gesturing towards the chair positioned directly in front of his large mahogany desk.

"Good morning, sir. You were looking for me?"

"Yes, thanks for coming up so promptly. I understand you have a Gregor Zanuk in custody being questioned over the killing of this banker chap, is that right?" Heffernan said.

"Yes, that's right, sir. Sergeant Moore had the good sense to have him lifted at the airport. He's over in Pearse Street now."

"Yes, I see. The problem is I've had a call from Foreign Affairs – no less than the Minister's private secretary. They're not happy. He prattled on for quite a long time about the importance of good relations with our European neighbours, and how Zanuk's company had millions invested in Ireland, blah blah blah."

"I see. Did you tell him that our neighbourly investment manager may well have conspired to murder three of our citizens?"

"Well, I didn't have that level of detail, Aidan, but I assured him that we wouldn't be holding Zanuk without very good reason," Heffernan said.

"And?"

"Like everything else, it's more complicated than it looks. The Minister is concerned, or so this fella said, that if Zanuk is charged, the whole thing will come out in the press, and Ireland's reputation as a safe place to invest money and manage overseas investments will be tarnished. You know yourself that banking is largely about confidence, and we're only just getting back on our feet after the meltdown in 2008."

"Are you telling me I have to let this turkey go?"

"I'm not telling you anything, Aidan. You're the SIO on these cases – it's your decision how you want to play it. I'm just repeating what has been said to me. But I can see the Minister's point though, can't you?" Heffernan said.

"Not really, sir. I deal with crime and criminals, not politics. If I can get Zanuk on conspiracy to murder, he'll serve a good few years here with us in Mountjoy. That's my objective."

"How strong is your evidence? After all, it would be a dreadful spectacle if we charged him and then he wasn't actually convicted. I can tell you, we could all watch out after something like that!"

"So, what do you want me to do?"

"Try and look at the broader picture. From what I hear, you have this other fella – what's his name?"

"Cotter, sir, Derek Cotter."

"Yes, Cotter, for two murders, so he'll be taken care of. Think of the ramifications for the National Bank. If all this gets exposed in the media, they'll lose all that business. Tens, maybe hundreds of jobs will be lost, and Ireland will be seen as a haven for hot Russian money, so no legitimate investors will trust us again for a long time. Is Zanuk really worth all that?"

Burke said nothing. He was processing what his senior officer had said. It went badly against the grain for him to let Zanuk go, but maybe, just maybe, he could reconcile it in his own head given the overall scenario.

"Let me think about it, sir. I just need an hour or so."

"Righto. But before you do anything dramatic, please inform me, OK?"

"Yes, of course, sir."

* * *

Burke left the station and headed back towards Pearse Street. He needed a drink. He stopped into Mulligan's in Poolbeg Street and ordered a pint of Guinness and a large whiskey. As he worked his way swiftly through the drinks, a plan began to form in his mind. By the time he had finished both, he was feeling a lot better.

Back at Pearse Street, he hooked up with Moore again.

"What did the boss want?"

"You'll see. Just follow my lead, OK?"

"OK, sure."

Back in the interview room, Moore was amazed at what Burke did next.

"Right, Mr Zanuk. You're free to leave. I'm very sorry for detaining you – clearly a misunderstanding on our part. There's a car from your embassy waiting outside to take you to the airport, and we'll make sure you get on the next available flight to Sofia."

"I should think so too," Zanuk said, getting up and putting on his jacket.

"And I want to take my knife," he added.

"We'd just like to keep that here for a few more days, Mr Zanuk. I'll make sure it is sent on to you in the diplomatic bag when we have finished with it. You have my word."

"OK, thanks, Inspector. No hard feelings." Zanuk extended his hand, and Burke had no option but to shake it.

"Thank you for being so understanding. Have a safe journey back to Bulgaria."

Zanuk was shown out to the waiting limousine. The chauffeur opened the rear door and Zanuk disappeared inside. The car then took off at speed towards the airport.

"What the hell was all that about?" Moore asked when they were walking back to Store Street.

"Ah, don't worry, Fiona, I'm not quite finished with Mr Zanuk yet. But Heffernan had taken a call from the pols, and was all agitated. You know what he's like when they are breathing down his neck. Anyway, when we get back, charge Cotter with everything you've got and for God sake, put that bloody knife away somewhere safe."

"By the way, what about your paint job?" Moore said.

"Oh, yeah, I'd forgotten all about that. I have the paint and all the kit now. Are you on for Saturday?"

"Yeah, sure. I'll call down at around eleven."

"Great, thanks."

Chapter Thirty-Two

Burke called Heffernan and told him that Zanuk was on his way back to the airport in an embassy car, and that he had been released without charge.

"Excellent, Aidan. I knew I could rely on you to do the right thing. Well done."

When he had finished talking to his boss, Burke looked through the address book he kept on his desk. He did have a modern smartphone, but he preferred to keep his contacts on paper. He selected a number from the little book, and dialled.

"Hi, Peter, it's Aidan Burke here. How's things?"

"Ah, Aidan. Good man, I hear you've been dabbling in a bit of banking lately. What's the story?"

Burke told his contact the plan that he had dreamt up while he was downing a couple of drinks in Mulligan's earlier.

"God, what they say about you, Burke, is all true, you crafty bugger. OK. Let me make a phone call or two. I won't come back to you, if that's all right, but you'll read about it in the papers in a week or two."

"Excellent. Thanks, Peter. I owe you one."

"All part of the service."

* * *

Moore turned up as promised at Burke's house the following Saturday in scruffy jeans and a T-shirt that had lots of paint stains on it.

When he opened the door to her, he said, "Christ – you didn't tell me you were a professional painter, Fiona!"

"Feck off, Aidan. I hope you have the coffee on, I've had no breakfast."

"Come in. I'll see what I've got in the cupboard."

What he had in the cupboard turned out to be pretty meagre. They just about managed to make two mugs of passable coffee, but the milk was off, and there were no biscuits or anything else to go with it.

"Jesus, Aidan," Moore said, "you need to start looking after yourself properly, or if you can't manage that, get yourself a woman."

"Sure, didn't I have one of those? Bloody fleeced me and all. I don't need any more of that, thank you very much. I'll be fine. I've cut back a lot on the booze, you know. I'm getting myself sorted out."

Moore had to admit that Burke's frequent absences from work while he nipped out to the pub for a few pints had reduced, in fact they were almost eliminated now. He was more careful about his appearance too. He rarely came to work unshaved these days, and his new clothes were smart and much more professional looking. She thought to herself that sober, and properly turned out, he was a fine figure of a man.

The two of them worked on quietly through the morning spreading the new paint evenly on the downstairs walls, occasionally standing back to admire their handiwork. Moore took the trickier bits around the door frames and windows, while Burke did the large plain areas with his roller. By one-thirty they had the front room totally refreshed, and looking a lot less tired than it had done previously.

"I suppose I'd better buy you lunch, Sergeant," Burke said.

"I suppose you had," she agreed. "Where are you taking me?"

"Nowhere posh looking like that anyway. How about the greasy spoon down the road on the corner? I could murder double egg and chips."

"God, you really know how to spoil a girl, don't you?" she replied, but she was laughing too. Burke was right – in their painting gear, with their faces and arms splashed with emulsion, they would not have been welcomed anywhere else.

Having had their surprisingly tasty lunch, they worked on through the afternoon finishing the hall. The place was now looking a lot brighter, and it smelled fresher too, the mustiness now having been overtaken by the smell of fresh paint.

At four o'clock, they decided to call it a day. They tidied up the dust sheets, washed out the brushes and rollers and put the lids firmly back on the part-used cans.

When the stuff was all cleared away, Moore got ready to leave.

"Right then, I'll be off. See you Monday," she said moving towards the door.

As she reached up to open the front door, Burke took her gently by the arm and turned her towards him.

"Listen, thanks so much, Fiona. You really have given me a boost, and I don't just mean the painting. I appreciate it a lot." Then he drew her to him and hugged her.

The embrace didn't last very long. When they separated, she didn't quite know what to say, so she just turned back to the door, opened it and exited to the road where her car was parked. As she drove away, she waved to Burke who was still standing in the doorway, and smiled broadly.

"God, what next?" she asked herself as she merged with the traffic. She had no idea how she felt after that encounter, but she knew she felt something, and it wasn't unpleasant. She wondered what her mother would make of this development!

* * *

Cotter had been brought to court charged with murder, and had been remanded in custody while the Gardaí prepared their book of evidence.

On the following Friday, Burke came into the office carrying, of all things, a copy of the Financial Times.

"Wait till you see this, Fiona," he said to her beckoning her into his office.

'Bulgarian Investment Company closed by the authorities. Bulgarian banking regulators have closed down the offices of Hastavia, a large investment firm in Sofia, citing irregularities in their dealings and suspected money laundering. The owner of the company, Gregor Zanuk, is helping the authorities with their investigation, but sources say that it is likely he will be charged and could face several years in jail. Hastavia is an international operation, with dealings right across Europe and in Russia.'

"And I don't suppose you had anything at all to do with that, sir?"

"Me? How could you possible suggest such a thing? Now, Sergeant. There's another matter that we have to discuss."

"Oh-oh. Am I in trouble?"

"No. On the contrary. I need to take you to dinner to thank you properly for your efforts last weekend. Somewhere posh and expensive. You choose. Saturday night, OK?"

"Well, if you insist, sir, that would be very nice. And I promise not to wear my painting gear!"

As she left the room, Fiona Moore wondered how all that might work out.

Character List

Detective Inspector Aidan Burke – a tough cop brought up on the streets of Dublin, who has his own particular style that doesn't always sit well with his superiors.

Detective Sergeant Fiona Moore – an enthusiastic detective who originally joined the force to find a man, but got more than she bargained for.

Superintendent Jerome Heffernan – head of the Detective Unit who treads a fine line between his men and the politicians.

Detective Dónal Lawlor – a young detective Garda who shows a lot of promise.

John McKenna – a young banker with a bright future, but some serious character flaws.

Pat and Mary McKenna – John's parents who are living in the 1950s.

Emma Rowe – a bank clerk who has fallen for McKenna's charms.

Irene – Emma's flatmate.

Mark – Sergeant Moore's cousin who works for a large investment bank in London.

Dr O'Higgins – the pathologist.

Anthony (Anto) O'Dowd – a rough diamond who operates in the shadows of Dublin's underworld.

Derek Cotter – a financial broker who turns rogue.

Gregor Zanuk – runs an investment company in Bulgaria.

Edmund Giltrap – a timid banker who has some unnecessary complications in his otherwise hum-drum life.

Jane Langford – works with the Garda Technical Bureau.

Conor Griffin – a barman who discovers more than he bargained for when he puts out the rubbish.

Dr Patel – an emergency doctor.

Peter Byrne – a forensics officer.

Dr Khatri – works in an all-night pharmacy.

Other characters:

Garda Richard Walsh; Garda Emily O'Connor; Jim Roberts from the forensics team.

If you enjoyed this book, please let others know by leaving a quick review on Amazon. Also, if you spot anything untoward in the paperback, get in touch. We strive for the best quality and appreciate reader feedback.

editor@thebookfolks.com

www.thebookfolks.com

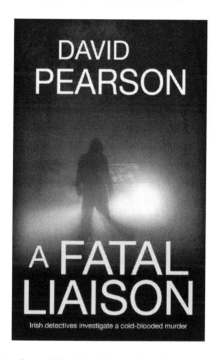

A man is found dead in his car in a forest outside of Dublin. Very dead. There is quite a mess. The police suspect foul play and call in the detectives. It is not long before another body is found in the area. A full-scale murder inquiry is launched. Can DI Aidan Burke and DS Fiona Moore collar the killer?

OTHER BOOKS BY DAVID PEARSON

In the Galway Homicides series:

Murder on the Old Bog Road (Book 1)
Murder at the Old Cottage (Book 2)
Murder on the West Coast (Book 3)
Murder at the Pony Show (Book 4)
Murder on Pay Day (Book 5)
Murder in the Air (Book 6)
Murder at the Holiday Home (Book 7)
Murder on the Peninsula (Book 8)
Murder at the Races (Book 9)

Available in paperback and free with Kindle Unlimited

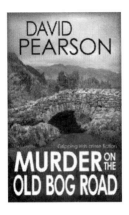

A woman is found in a ditch, murdered. As the list of suspects grows, an Irish town's dirty secrets are exposed. Detective Inspector Mick Hays and DS Maureen Lyons are called in to investigate. But getting the locals to even speak to the police will take some doing. Will they find the killer in their midst?

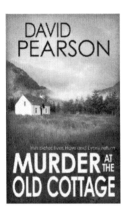

When a nurse finds a reclusive old man dead in his armchair in his cottage, the local Garda surmise he was the victim of a burglary gone wrong. However, having suffered a violent death and there being no apparent robbery, Irish detectives are not so sure. It will take all their wits and training to track down the killer.

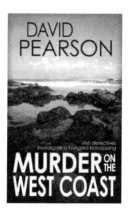

When the Irish police arrive at a road accident, they find evidence of a kidnapping and a murder. Detective Maureen Lyons is in charge of the case but, struggling with self-doubt, when a suspect slips through her fingers she must act fast to save her reputation and crack the case.

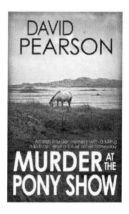

A man is found dead during the annual Connemara Pony Show. Panic spreads through the event when it is discovered he was murdered. Detective Maureen Lyons leads the investigation but the powers that be threaten to stonewall the inquiry.

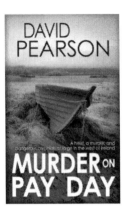

Following a tip-off, Irish police lie in wait for a robbery. But the criminals cleverly evade their grasp. Meanwhile, a body is found beneath a cliff. DCI Mick Hays' chances of promotion will be blown unless he sorts out the mess.

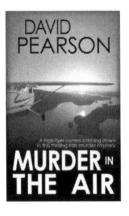

After a wealthy businessman's plane crashes into bogland it is discovered the engine was tampered with. But who out of the three occupants was the intended target? DI Maureen Lyons leads the investigation, which points to shady dealings and an even darker crime.

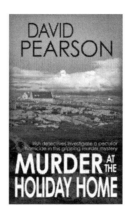

A local businessman is questioned when a young woman is found dead in his property. His caginess makes him a prime suspect in what is now a murder inquiry. But with no clear motive and no evidence, detectives will have a hard task proving their case. They'll have to follow the money, even if it leads them into danger.

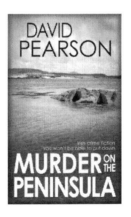

When a body is found on a remote Irish beach, detectives suspect foul play. Their investigation leads them to believe the death is connected to corruption in local government. But rather than have to hunt down the killer, he approaches them. With one idea in mind: revenge.

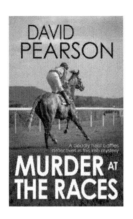

One of the highlights of Ireland's horseracing calendar is marred when a successful bookmaker is robbed and killed in the restrooms. DI Maureen Lyons investigates but is not banking on a troublemaker emerging from within the police ranks. Her team will have to deal with the shenanigans and catch a killer.

Printed in Poland
by Amazon Fulfillment
Poland Sp. z o.o., Wrocław

60167901R00125